THE STUBBORN FATHER

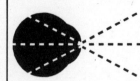

THE STUBBORN FATHER

WANDA E. BRUNSTETTER AND JEAN BRUNSTETTER

THORNDIKE PRESS

A part of Gale, Cengage Learning

GALE
CENGAGE Learning·

Farmington Hills, Mich • San Francisco • New York • Waterville, Maine
Meriden, Conn • Mason, Ohio • Chicago

GALE
CENGAGE Learning®

LIBRARY OF CONGRESS CATALOGING-IN-PUBLICATION DATA

Names: Brunstetter, Wanda E., author. | Brunstetter, Jean, author.
Title: The stubborn father / by Wanda E Brunstetter and Jean Brunstetter.
Description: Large print edition. | Waterville, Maine : Thorndike Press, 2016. | © 2016 | Series: The Amish millionaire ; part 2 of 6 | Series: Thorndike Press large print Christian fiction
Identifiers: LCCN 2016009913| ISBN 9781410487988 (hardcover) | ISBN 1410487989 (hardcover)
Subjects: LCSH: Amish—Pennsylvania—Lancaster County—Fiction. | Large type books. | GSAFD: Christian fiction.
Classification: LCC PS3602.R864 S78 2016 | DDC 813/.6—dc23
LC record available at http://lccn.loc.gov/2016009913

Published in 2016 by arrangement with Barbour Publishing, Inc.

Printed in Mexico
1 2 3 4 5 6 7 20 19 18 17 16

THE STUBBORN FATHER

BYLER FAMILY TREE

Eustace and Effie (deceased) Byler's Children

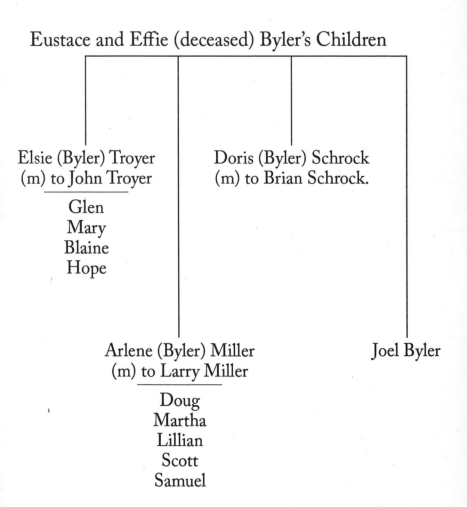

Elsie (Byler) Troyer
(m) to John Troyer

Glen
Mary
Blaine
Hope

Doris (Byler) Schrock
(m) to Brian Schrock.

Arlene (Byler) Miller
(m) to Larry Miller

Doug
Martha
Lillian
Scott
Samuel

Joel Byler

CHAPTER 1

Charm, Ohio

"That son of mine can sure get under my skin," Eustace grumbled, pacing the living-room floor. Never once had Joel apologized for the hurt he'd caused his family by leaving the Amish church. Even worse, he only came around whenever he wanted something and didn't act interested in being part of their family. With the exception of Eustace's eight-year-old grandson, Scott, Joel had hardly spoken to anyone during his visit here tonight. It would have been nice if Joel had actually stayed the night and the two of them could have visited like any normal father and son. But no, Joel let his temper get the best of him and stormed out the door.

Guess I can't blame him, though. Joel was upset because I wouldn't loan him twenty-five thousand dollars. Eustace frowned. *It was a lot of money to ask for — an amount Joel would probably never pay back.*

It wasn't because Eustace didn't have adequate funds in the bank — he had more than enough to loan Joel. *But if I'd given it to him, what would it teach my selfish son? He has to learn responsibility sometime in his life. After all, he's twenty-six years old.*

Eustace stopped pacing and stared at his wife's old rocking chair, empty and void without her. "This is your fault, Effie." He pointed at the chair as if she were sitting there. "Our son has become ungrateful for everything we've done for him. You spoiled him rotten from the time he was born."

Eustace stood by Effie's chair, using his foot to get it rocking in motion. As the chair creaked back and forth, he could almost see his wife looking defiantly back at him. The more he thought about what Effie would have said if she were there, the more he had to admit she'd probably be right. After having three daughters, Eustace had been so excited to have a boy when Joel came along that he'd been a bit too permissive as well. He'd often looked the other way when Joel had done something he shouldn't, and he'd given him things he probably didn't need.

In some ways Joel reminded Eustace of himself. As a youngster he'd been full of energy, anxious to explore the world, and always looking to try new things.

But I was grounded in my faith. Eustace sat down in Effie's rocker, grasping the arms of the chair. *Well, at least in most things. I stayed true to my church and family. That's more than Joel can say.*

Eustace's gaze came to rest on the Bible lying on the small table beside him. Effie's Bible. When the children were all living at home, their mother would gather them around the rocking chair every evening while she read a passage of scripture out loud. Then after the children were grown and out on their own, she'd read to Eustace. Afterward, they would discuss the verses and how they applied to their life. Eustace missed those days. He missed everything about his dear wife and all they'd done together. He and Effie had been deeply in love, and he'd never grown tired of learning more about her.

Because Effie is gone doesn't mean I should neglect Bible reading. Eustace picked up her Bible and opened it to a section in the book of Luke she'd marked with a white ribbon. Holding the book made him feel closer to Effie. He noticed the page had several verses underlined — in fact, a whole passage about the prodigal son that started at verse 11 of chapter 15.

A lump formed in Eustace's throat as he read the story. Joel was like the prodigal, only he had never come back repentant. His vision blurred, and his heart ached for his son. *He needs to repent, Lord,* Eustace prayed. *Even if Joel never comes back to live as an Amish man, I hope he will find his way back to You. If there is anything I can do to help my son see the error of his ways, please show me how.*

Wiping tears with his shirtsleeve,

he murmured, "My job as Joel's father is to help him get on the right path. Effie would agree with me wholeheartedly on that. My *kinner* are too important for me to look the other way. As long as there is breath in my body, I need to keep looking for a way."

He sat staring at the Bible then closed his eyes for a while. Finally, an idea popped into his head. It might not be the right thing to do, and perhaps Joel would never change, but at least Eustace could find solace in making an attempt to bring Joel to the Lord. Rising from Effie's chair, he turned off the gas lamp and made his way down the hall to get ready for bed.

Dover, Ohio

"Wh–where am I?" Joel moaned when someone's cold fingers touched his forehead. "Kristi, is that you?" He was surprised when he opened his eyes long enough to see a middle-aged woman with short brown hair looking down at him. *What's going on here?*

"You're in the hospital. Please lie still. I'm Karen, your nurse and I need to take your vitals now. Dr. Blake, your attending physician, doesn't want you to try and get up yet."

This couldn't be true, even though Joel's body hurt in places he didn't know he had. A small attempt to shift his weight made every muscle scream out in pain.

"Wh–what happened? How'd I get here?"

"You were in an accident and brought here to Union Hospital by ambulance." Her touch was gentle as she lifted Joel's arm and took his blood pressure.

"Oh, yeah, now I remember." Joel squeezed his eyes shut as he attempted to block out the pain. "A crazy driver swerved into my lane and came straight at me. I'll bet he was drunk." Joel moaned, a little deeper this time. "How bad am I hurt? Was there much damage to my truck?"

"Your condition isn't serious, but you do have a mild concussion, so we are keeping you overnight for observation. If you're having a lot of pain, we can give you something to help. I'll get in touch with the doctor and see what he will allow for the discomfort." The nurse gently patted his arm. "Try to rest now. The doctor will be in to see you soon."

"But what about my truck?"

"I'm not sure, sir. I imagine a tow truck was called, so your vehicle was probably taken to the impound yard."

"Great." Joel grunted in frustration, turning his head to the side. "Where's my cell phone? I need to make a call."

Speaking softly, the nurse replied, "When you were brought to this room, only your clothes and wallet were with you."

"I have to call Kristi so I can let her know what's happened. Maybe she can find my car, and my cell phone, too."

"Is Kristi a relative?"

"No, she's my girlfriend. I don't have any family. At least none who care about me." Joel couldn't keep the bitterness from his tone. After the way he'd been treated at Dad's tonight, he didn't care if he ever saw any of his family again.

"There's a telephone right here you can use to call your girlfriend." She gestured to the phone near his bed.

A searing pain shot through Joel's head as he shook it vigorously. "Her number is programmed into my cell phone, and I don't have it memorized."

"If she has a landline, we can look it up in the phone directory."

Joel clenched his teeth, which also made his head hurt. "It's a good idea, but Kristi only has a cell phone." A sense of panic rose in his soul. He felt trapped here in the hospital with no cell phone, unable to get ahold of Kristi. Joel needed her now, more than ever.

Akron, Ohio

"I appreciate you coming over to help me today." Kristi Palmer's mother smiled and leaned on her hoe. "These weeds are getting the best of my garden, and since your dad's back is hurting, he's not up to helping right now."

Kristi dug her shovel into the ground. "I'm glad I could do it, Mom. Since Joel spent the night out of town somewhere, I won't be seeing him until later today."

"I figured he must be doing something else, or you would have been with him, like you are most Saturdays." Mom's tone wasn't sharp, but Kristi sensed an underlying message. Her mother had made her views on Joel quite clear. She didn't approve of Kristi's boyfriend and thought she spent too much time with him.

Kristi's throat felt dry as she swallowed. "I'm going in for a drink; my throat's parched. Want me to bring you something when I come back out?"

"I wouldn't mind a glass of lemonade. Help yourself to some. I made it fresh this morning."

"Thanks, Mom. I'll check on Dad while I'm in there."

When Kristi entered the house, she picked up her cell phone, which she'd left on the kitchen counter, and glanced at the message icon to see if Joel may have called or sent a text. No messages showed, so apparently he hadn't tried to get in touch with her.

He's probably not back yet. Or he might have gotten busy with something and forgotten to call. Maybe I should call him.

After checking on her father, Kristi went back outside with the lemonade and her cell phone.

"Here you go, Mom."

Mom smiled and reached for the glass.

Kristi took a gulp of the cold liquid. "This sure tastes good. Do you want to take a break while we cool off?"

"You go ahead if you want to. I'm going to keep working." Mom tucked a wayward strand of hair behind her ear. "I'll join you after I pull a couple of these more stubborn weeds. Some of them feel like their roots go all the way to China."

Kristi smiled as Mom set her glass down to play tug-of-war with a weed. Mom could also be stubborn, so those weeds didn't have a chance.

Taking a seat on the grass, Kristi

punched in Joel's number. When it went to his voice mail, she left a message. "Hi, Joel, it's me. Just wondered if you're still out of town or back home by now. I'm at my mom's, helping in the garden, but I'll be home sometime this afternoon. So give me a call when you can and we'll make plans for later."

For the next few hours, Kristi kept busy pulling weeds and then picking green beans and cucumbers. Mom's garden had done quite well this year, even with the weeds threatening to take over. Kristi wished she could have a garden of her own, but living in a condo with only a deck didn't allow for growing much of anything. Kristi had managed to squeeze in a few pots of flowers on the deck, but a barbecue grill, small table, and two chairs took up the rest of the space.

Someday when she and Joel got married, she would have plenty of space for gardening. Joel had two acres of land. Even with his single-wide mobile home, garage, and shop, his yard had plenty of room for a garden as well as fruit trees. She was glad he'd chosen to live outside of town and not in the city like she did.

Of course, being in the city had some advantages. In addition to being closer to stores for shopping, Kristi worked at a nursing home not far from her condo. She'd have to commute once she and Joel were married, but it was a small trade-

off. Having grown up in the sub-
urbs of Akron, where Mom and
Dad still lived, she had always
longed to live in the country.

Kristi reflected on the trip she
and Mom had taken nearly a
month ago to Holmes County. The
best part of the weekend had been
seeing all the Amish buggies,
homes, and farms in the area. She'd
heard that Holmes County had the
largest population of Amish in
America, and tourism was on the
rise every year. If Kristi had her
way, she would live among the
Amish, but moving there would be
too far from her job. Besides, Joel
had shown no interest in even visiting Amish country, so she was sure
he'd never agree to move there.

Kristi brushed the dirt from her gloves and stood. "It's almost noon, Mom. Should we stop and have lunch? I'd like to try calling Joel again, too."

Mom wiped her forehead with the back of her hand. "Stopping's a good idea. We've done enough work for one day." She rose to her feet. "I'll go in and start lunch while you make your call."

After Mom went inside, Kristi called Joel again. Still no answer, so she left another message. She tried not to worry, but couldn't shake the feeling that something was wrong. *Please, Lord,* she prayed, *keep Joel safe, wherever he is. And let me hear something from him soon.*

CHAPTER 2

Charm

Eustace sat at the kitchen table, staring at the untouched bowl of soup he'd heated for lunch. It was hard to eat alone. *Maybe I should have gone into town and had my meal at the newly opened restaurant owned by an Amish family,* he thought, rocking the ketchup bottle back and forth with his hands. *I may have run into someone from the community who could have sat at my table. It would sure beat sittin' here alone. If I'd been thinking, I would have called my New Order friend, Henry, and asked him to meet me there.*

Eustace got up and poured the soup from his bowl back into the pot. Once it cooled off, he'd refrigerate the soup to have another day. Soup season was fast approaching. Over the winter months, any kind of soup was good, as long as it was hot.

He walked out to the porch and breathed deeply of the September air. Where had the time gone? Resting against the porch post, Eustace viewed the swaying trees along the back of his property as soft winds blew past the area. The leaves from the branches fell delicately, like feathers, to the smooth lawn. A smile crossed Eustace's face. *Maybe I can work up a better appetite if I take a walk.*

Eustace headed straight for the tree line. *No better time than the present to pick out the tree where I'll build Effie's tree house.*

Many large trees, especially maple and oak, silhouetted the azure sky. As Eustace walked from tree to tree, he came upon one of the largest: a huge maple standing quite high, with branches jutting out in every direction. This tree had been there since the children were little, and even then it had seemed tall. Many times Effie packed a picnic basket, and the family enjoyed lunch under the shade of its branches.

Eustace stood at the base and looked up. *The view from those branches must be beautiful,* he thought.

Luckily, the tree had enough low-lying branches he could easily latch on to. As he pondered what to do next, the urge to climb won out. Reaching toward the first limb, Eustace was surprised at how effortless it was to get up on it.

Climbing from one branch to the next highest was easier than he expected. Each time he stopped to get a good foothold, he surveyed the landscape. *Maybe the next branch will give an ever better view.*

Midway up, he came to a spot where many branches on the sides and back part of the tree cradled toward the middle, giving him a wider area to stand on. The front had an ample opening. Eustace knew immediately that this was the perfect tree. He leaned back against the main part of the trunk, which at this height was still quite wide.

No wonder Effie wanted to be up here with the birds, he mused, looking out over their property. From here, Eustace could see the entire farm, the rolling fields where his horses lazily fed, and the hill his son used to venture to when he wanted to be by himself. Joel had never been aware anyone else knew of his special place on the hill. Eustace never let on, respecting his son's need to be alone at times.

Without a doubt, Effie's tree house would be built here. He looked toward the sky at a big puffy cloud and imagined his wife sitting upon it. "This is it, Effie. I found a perfect maple for your tree house."

Eustace's goal would be to have it finished before winter set in, so he could enjoy going up there without fear of snow. His excitement grew. Now he'd have a project to do, keeping him busy for the next several weeks.

Guess I better get back to the house. Maybe I'll put the soup away and head into town to try out the new restaurant. I'm gettin' kinda hungry.

Eustace pushed himself away from the tree, but didn't get far. Something felt wrong. Why couldn't he move from the spot where he stood? Something was keeping him in place. Moving this way and that, but to no avail, Eustace suddenly realized his suspenders had gotten hooked on something behind him. He tried reaching back to undo whatever he was caught on, but unfortunately it was out of reach. *Now what in tarnation am I gonna do?*

Eustace's thoughts halted when he heard a whinny off in the distance, followed by the faint *clip-clop* of a horse's hooves coming up the driveway. From his vantage point, he saw his eldest daughter, Elsie, climb down from her buggy.

Cupping his hands around his mouth, Eustace yelled, to get his daughter's attention. He saw her stop and look in all directions, but she hadn't spied him yet. Next, he gave out a shrill whistle. After a few more tries, she finally heard him. He watched as Elsie quickly tied the horse and sprinted up to the tree, now holding him prisoner. "What are you doing, Dad? You're up there pretty high, aren't you?"

"I'll explain later. Right now, I need your help. I'm stuck on something." Eustace pointed toward his back. "Do you think you can climb up and help me? As I recall, you used to love climbing trees when you were little, and I made it up here pretty easily myself."

"You're talkin' years ago, Dad, but I'll give it a try."

Eustace watched his daughter start climbing, as if she were a little girl again. Soon, she made her way up, smiling when she stood next to him. The spot had enough room for them to stand side-by-side.

"See here." Eustace leaned forward. "It seems my suspenders are caught on something. I couldn't reach around to get them unhooked."

"Somehow you got one suspender strap caught on a notch in the tree where a branch snapped off, possibly years ago."

"Thought I felt something digging into my back, but the view up here was so wonderful, I ignored it."

Eustace was glad Elsie had no

trouble undoing his suspender. "*Danki,* Daughter. You came in the nick of time."

"You can tell me why you are up here later. What I want to know now is why didn't you simply unhook your suspenders from the front of your trousers?" Elise looked at him quizzically. "You would have been freed immediately."

"I didn't think of it." Eustace snickered. "Now that you mention it, I feel kinda silly."

"Let's get you out of this tree and back to the house."

As they walked arm-in-arm toward the farm, Eustace looked at his daughter. "Danki again for coming to my aid." He gave Elsie's hand a squeeze. "Now how about some lunch? I have potato soup to reheat."

"Soup sounds good, but I brought us some sandwiches." They paused by her buggy, and while Eustace petted her horse, Elsie drew out a wicker basket.

"We can have both." Eustace smiled as they approached the house. Now he wouldn't have to eat alone. All three of his daughters were good to him and, for some reason, usually sensed when it was time to drop by. He was sure whatever kind of sandwiches she'd made would be good, because, like her mom, Elsie was an excellent cook.

"I brought a jug of tea along, too." Elsie went to the kitchen sink to wash her hands.

"Is it sweetened?"

She shook her head. "But feel free to add sugar if you like."

"Think I will." Eustace opened the cupboard and took out the sugar, while Elsie got the glasses and went to the freezer for some ice. Gasping, she jumped backward. "Dad, what is this huge thing wrapped in a clear bag? Is — is it a dead bird?"

"Now don't start fussing. It's a pheasant I found dead this morning. I'll be taking it to my friend who does taxidermy later, but wanted to make sure it stayed fresh."

Elsie groaned. "Do you really need a stuffed pheasant? I mean, where are you planning to put it?"

"Don't rightly know, but I'm sure I'll find a place for the bird."

Elsie opened her mouth as if to say something more, but then she grabbed the ice cube tray, shut the freezer door, and came back to the table. Eustace sensed she thought his decision to keep the pheasant was weird. Well, she could keep her opinion to herself. This was his house, and he could do whatever he wanted.

Elsie frowned as she sat across the table from her father. The wrinkles across his forehead seemed more pronounced than usual, and his shoulders were slumped.

"Guess you're wondering what I

was doing up in the tree." Dad looked tired as she smiled at him. "I found the perfect place to build your *mamm*'s tree house."

"Do you think it's still a good idea, since Mama isn't here to enjoy it?"

"You probably see it as pointless, but it's something I feel the need to do. Besides, it'll keep me busy during the lonely times."

"But Dad, the cold seasons are coming soon, and what about snow?"

"I'll take advantage of the nice days we're having now." He heaved a sigh. "It'll keep my mind off other things."

Elsie saw no point in arguing with

her father. He had his mind made up.

"Is anything else wrong, Dad?" She took a bite of her soup. "You look kind of *umgerennt* this afternoon — like something might be bothering you."

He nodded. "You're right; there is. I'm upset with Joel."

"Didn't things go well when he spent the night?"

"No, they did not, and he didn't stay." Dad grabbed the bottle of ketchup and squeezed some into his soup, which was nothing unusual for him. With the exception of desserts and fruit, he liked ketchup on nearly everything he ate.

"What happened? Why didn't Joel

stay overnight like he'd planned?"

"He left because I wouldn't give him what he wanted." Dad's eyes narrowed and his nostrils flared like a charging bull. "I should have realized he only came here to ask for money. Joel's exasperating and selfish. He doesn't give a hoot about his family."

"Exasperating? Is that another word you found in your dictionary?"

Dad's eyes widened; then he lowered his voice. "How did you know about my dictionary?"

"I've walked past you a couple of times while you were reading it. I'm surprised you never noticed."

"Oh, I see. Well as I was saying, Joel had no intention of trying to amend things with us. I can't remember the last time he didn't come over to ask me for money."

Elsie fidgeted with her hands underneath the table. "If you don't mind me asking, what does Joel need money for?"

"He didn't go into detail, but it was something about owing his subcontractors." Dad's thick brows furrowed. "Guess he must not be runnin' a good business if he's gettin' himself in over his head."

Elsie felt concern for her brother. "Maybe we should all chip in and help him out."

Dad's hand came down hard on the table, causing some soup to spill out of his bowl. "Absolutely not! I've bailed your brother out before, and look where it got me. It didn't teach Joel a thing about responsibility, and he never even bothered to pay back the loan." Dad rolled his chair across the floor and grabbed a roll of paper towels; then he rolled back to the table and wiped up his mess.

After they finished eating their lunch, Dad sat looking out the window. Elsie wondered if he was still thinking about Joel. When she slid out of her chair and rose to start clearing their plates, Dad reached over and grabbed both of their bowls. Then he rolled across the room and placed them in the kitchen sink. Without a word, he rolled back to the table and grabbed his drink.

Elsie poured liquid dish soap into the sink and turned on the water, trying to hide her smile. Watching Dad roll his chair across the floor always made her giggle. It was something he'd done since she was a child.

A few seconds later, she heard the back screen door open and close. When she heard a familiar squeak, she knew Dad had made himself comfortable on the porch swing. While the sink filled with sudsy water, Elsie unwrapped the new sponge she'd brought along today. She wasn't surprised to discover Dad's old sponge lying near the back of the sink. For some reason, he couldn't part with the old thing. Of course, it was one of many things Dad couldn't let go of.

When the dishes were washed, dried, and put away, Elsie poured herself more tea and went outside to join Dad. Taking a seat beside him on the swing, she sat quietly, mulling things over. She felt bad Joel had gotten himself in a bind, but was also concerned for her father. She was sure Dad loved his son as much as he did his daughters. Saying no to Joel's request must have been hard, even if Dad felt he was doing the right thing. It wasn't likely Joel would ever return to the Amish faith, but if he'd come by once in a while to be with his family, things would go better between him and Dad. Joel also needed to be true to his word and pay back any money he'd previously borrowed.

Dover

"I'm not hungry," Joel grunted, pushing aside the lunch tray a young woman had brought into his hospital room.

She smiled. "It's okay; I'll leave it here in case you change your mind."

"I won't, so you may as well take it away."

With a slight shrug, she picked up the tray and started out of the room.

"Say, wait. Would you see if you can find me a phone book for Summit County? I need to make a call, and I don't know the number."

"I'll see what I can do." She smiled and hurried from the room.

Trying not to let his agitation get the best of him, Joel glanced out the window to his left. The sun shone brightly in a blue sky accented by a couple of puffy white clouds. It was too nice a day to be cooped up in a stuffy hospital room. When the doctor had come in that morning to check on Joel, he said that Joel could probably go home before the day was out, but they were still waiting for a few more of his test results.

Don't think my accident would have happened if I'd spent the night at Dad's. Joel gripped the rails on his bed with such force that the veins on his hands stuck out. *I should have stayed there and tried to play on his sympathy instead of losing my temper and storming off. If I'd pled my case long and hard enough, Dad may have relented and loaned me the money I so desperately need. Now what am I supposed to do?*

Joel reached for the remote and turned on the TV. Even though he was now living the English way and owned his own TV, he'd never enjoyed watching most of the shows. Many of them made no sense and seemed like a waste of time. Still, maybe listening to something was better than nothing.

Joel scanned all the stations. Earlier, the aid had explained the hospital rooms were hooked up to cable, and he had many more channels to choose from, along with the local ones. Joel finally found a station, but the show was in black and white instead of color. It looked like an old movie, depicting a time back in the '50s. Joel didn't know about growing up in the '50s, but he'd heard plenty about it from his parents.

Even these days his family lived in their simple ways. The Amish had always lived plain, but the English world had changed. Back then, people didn't have cell phones, computers, video games, or tablets, and they talked rather than texted with each other. In today's world, it seemed Englishers always had some sort of gizmo or gadget in their hands. They were either texting someone or had a cell phone to their ear, even when they were driving. *Times were simpler for the English back then,* Joel thought as he watched the TV family sitting at the dinner table, talking. Although not easier by today's standards, he was sure they had to feel a sense of accomplishment when they worked hard like the Amish folks still did today.

Joel was getting more into the show when the aid bounded into the room. "Here you go, Mr. Byler — the phone book you requested."

Joel thanked her for responding to his request. He waited until she left the room, then proceeded to look up the number for Kristi's parents.

"Ah, here it is." He held one finger on the listing for Paul Palmer in Akron. "Sure hope someone's home so I don't have to leave a message."

Joel scooted the phone closer to his bed and punched in the number. He felt relief when Kristi's dad picked up.

"Palmer residence. This is Paul."

"Oh, hey, this is Joel. I'm in the hospital in Dover, and I need to talk to Kristi. Could you give me her cell number?"

"Sorry to hear you're in the hospital. Are you ill? Have you been hurt?"

"I was in a car accident last night, but my injuries aren't serious. Now about Kristi's number . . ."

"Kristi is here right now, Joel. She and JoAnn are in the kitchen fixing lunch. I'll go get her."

Joel compressed his lips while he waited several minutes, until he heard Kristi's voice on the phone. "Joel, are you all right? Dad said you were in an accident."

"Yeah, I was, and for the most part, I'm okay." Joel paused and drew in a quick breath. "I have no idea where my truck is, and my cell phone is missing. Kristi, I need you here with me. Can you come?"

"Of course, Joel. I'll leave right now, and if traffic isn't heavy, I should be there in less than an hour."

Joel breathed a sigh of relief. Once Kristi got here, everything would be okay. He wouldn't tell her where he'd gone last evening, though, or why he'd been heading home in the middle of the night.

CHAPTER 3

Akron

Joel tossed his classic car magazine aside. He had been home from the hospital a week, recuperating. Most of his time was spent lying on the couch, either staring at the TV or reading. While none of Joel's injuries had been serious, his muscles were stiff and sore, making him feel like he'd been trampled by a herd of horses. The headache brought on by the concussion still lingered, and Joel's ribs hurt whenever he took a deep breath or moved the wrong way.

Despite the pain, he couldn't stay around here indefinitely. He needed to round up more jobs and get some money coming in. Since Dad refused to give him a loan, Joel needed cash more than ever. Besides owing some of his men, Joel had a hospital bill and the repair of his truck to worry about. Even though the man who'd hit him had insurance, it could be awhile before Joel received a settlement, and he wasn't sure how much of his medical expenses would be covered. His own insurance would pay 80 percent of the hospital bill, but hopefully neither that nor his deductible would be needed when the other driver's insurance paid up.

Then there was the matter of his truck, which was in the shop getting repaired. Joel was relieved the truck hadn't been totaled. He needed it in order to keep working. Once he got it back from the shop, he hoped he'd be healed enough to begin working again. He had been told when he left the hospital to take it easy for a few weeks, which he wasn't thrilled about. No money coming in meant he'd be further in debt.

Joel tossed the magazine aside. *If only my dad weren't so stubborn and selfish. It's his fault I'm under so much stress. He could make my life easy if he'd give me the money, instead of being so stingy. I wonder if he'd treat my sisters the same way if they were in need. I thought Christians were supposed to be kind and giving.*

It did no good to get himself all worked up, so Joel closed his eyes and thought about the beautiful Corvette out in his shop. He imagined himself gripping the steering wheel at 70 mph on the freeway and hearing the engine roar as it accelerated. Joel would give almost anything to take his new beauty for a drive right now to forget all his troubles. At least nobody could steal his joy when he was behind the wheel.

Kristi would be coming by soon to fix his supper, as she'd been doing since he was released from the hospital. Joel glanced at his cell phone, thankful it had been found on the floor of his truck. *Maybe I should call and tell her not to come by. I'll say I have leftovers and don't need her to cook me anything this evening. It would give me the opportunity to take the Vette out.* Joel really wasn't up to it and shouldn't be thinking about the new car right now. What he needed was something to take his mind off things. He continued to worry about the money he'd taken from his and Kristi's joint savings account. If Kristi knew what he'd done, she'd never trust him again.

The unmistakable sound of Kristi's car interrupted his thoughts. Groaning from the pain in his ribs,

Joel pulled himself off the couch and walked stiffly across the room toward the front door, reaching it just as Kristi entered carrying a white sack.

"I hope you're in the mood for supreme burritos tonight, because I stopped at the Mexican restaurant near my condo and got take-out." She smiled up at him and lifted the bag. "I told you I'd cook something special, but since this is Saturday and I didn't have to work, the major part of my day was spent cleaning the house. By the time the chores were done, I was too tired to even think about cooking."

"Burritos are fine, Kristi." Joel motioned to the kitchen. "We can either eat them in there or sit out here in the living room." Joel didn't have a formal dining room in his small single-wide, so when he was alone, he often ate his meals in front of the TV.

Kristi shook her head. "I don't want to compete with the television. It makes it too hard for us to visit."

Joel shrugged his shoulders. "Okay, whatever. If you prefer, we can eat in the kitchen."

"You sound grumpy, Joel. If you'd rather eat out here, it's fine with me. I don't want to cause you more irritation. Let's not turn on the TV, though, okay?"

"It doesn't matter where we eat. I'm irritable because I'm tired of sittin' around here when I should be working. I need money, and none will come in unless I get out there and beat the bushes." He stepped into the kitchen and got out some napkins and paper plates.

Kristi placed the burritos on the table and poured them both a glass of lemonade, which she'd taken from the refrigerator. "Why don't you take some money out of our joint account? After all, you've put money in there, too."

"Umm . . . I'd rather not." Joel felt like a bug trapped in a spider's web. No way could he admit he'd already taken money from their account to pay some of his debts. Truth was, only a small amount of money remained.

"It's okay," she insisted. "If you're

not feeling up to going out on Monday, I can stop by the bank on my way home from work and make a withdrawal. How much do you think you'll need?"

Joel's heart hammered in his chest. "No, Kristi, I am not touching our joint account. I'll be going back to work on Monday. I should have some money coming in soon." Joel's conscience pricked him. He should have been honest with Kristi in the beginning, but it seemed too late to explain. He had no choice now but to get back to work and try to put a little in the bank whenever he could. Since the monthly bank statements came to his house, hopefully, Kristi would never be aware of what had transpired.

■ ■ ■ ■

Charm

Arlene clucked to her horse to get him moving faster. At the rate the gelding had been plodding along it would be way past suppertime before she got to Dad's with the casserole she'd made. She hoped to find him in a good mood. Her sister Elsie had mentioned that when she'd dropped by to see Dad last week he'd been irritated with Joel. She'd said she needed to talk to her about something else, but wanted their sister, Doris, in on the conversation. Of course, their father's irritation with Joel was nothing new. Every time Joel's name was mentioned, Dad became uptight. If Joel came around asking for money, Dad's mood would sometimes be affected for weeks.

It was a shame he and Joel couldn't put their differences aside and enjoy each other's company. But Dad's stubbornness and un-willingness to forgive got in the way. Joel's disinterest in being part of the family didn't help, either. While Joel had a right to choose whether he wanted to be Amish or English, he should have made his choice before joining the church. Up until then, everyone thought Joel would marry Anna Detweiler and settle into married life.

Poor Anna. I wonder if she's ever gotten over Joel. Arlene couldn't imagine going through such rejection — especially when it happened only a few days before the wedding. Not only did Anna have to live through the embarrassment of having to call off the wedding at the last minute, but it must have hurt to know Joel didn't love her enough to remain Amish.

"It hurt us, too," Arlene mumbled, tapping the reins until her horse picked up speed again. *When Joel left, it grieved Mom and Dad most of all.*

Forcing her negative thoughts aside, Arlene snapped the reins once more. "Giddy-up, Buddy. Time's a-wastin'. We need to get to my *daed's* sometime today."

When Arlene finally guided her horse and buggy up Dad's driveway, smoke was pouring through the slightly open kitchen window.

She leaped from the buggy, secured Buddy to the hitching rail, and ran toward the house. Heart pounding, she raced inside, where more smoke billowed from the kitchen. Since it seemed to be isolated to that room, she figured something might be burning on the stove.

Removing her apron and waving it in front of her face, Arlene held her breath as she made her way across the room. Quickly opening the oven door, she realized whatever was baking had been reduced to nothing more than a blackened lump. Grabbing a potholder, she picked up the glass baking dish and carried it outside to the porch. Then she rushed back inside, turned off the oven, and opened the other two kitchen windows. The situation under control, Arlene cupped her hands around her mouth and shouted for Dad.

No response.

She ran through the house, checking in every room, but saw no sign of him. Since she hadn't seen him outside when she pulled in, Arlene figured he might be in the barn.

Sure enough, she found him there kneeling in front of an old milk can, holding a paint brush. "What did you have in the oven, Dad?" she panted. "Do you realize it's burned to a crisp?"

He whirled around, nearly dropping the brush. "Daughter, don't sneak up on me like that!"

"I wasn't sneaking. I'm surprised you didn't hear my horse and buggy pull in."

"Guess I was too deep in concentration to notice." He stood. "Now, what's this about my meatloaf burning?"

She squinted. "So it was meatloaf? It looks like a brick of charcoal now, and the kitchen's all *schmokich*. I could hardly breathe."

"I got so busy out here, I forgot to check on it." Grunting, Dad frowned. "So much for supper. Guess I'll have to fix a sandwich now."

"No, you won't. I brought you a chicken-and-rice casserole. It's in my buggy."

He smiled. "Danki. It was thoughtful of you. And it'll be a heap better than burned meatloaf."

Arlene pressed her hand to her mouth and puffed out her cheeks. "You'd never be able to eat it, Dad. What started out as a meatloaf is burned beyond recognition. And you know what else?"

He tipped his head. "What?"

"You could have burned down the whole house." She sighed deeply. "If you're determined to live here alone, then you need to stay in the house while your supper is cooking. Better yet, Doris, Elsie, and I can take turns either bringing your evening meal or having you to one of our homes to eat."

Dad shook his head. "There's no need for all the fuss, Arlene. You and your sisters do enough for me already. From now on, I'll stay inside whenever I'm cooking."

She pursed her lips. "You promise?"

"*Jah,* and to put your mind at ease, you'll be happy to know your aunt Verna is comin' next week for a visit. While she's here, she'll probably want to do all the cooking. Besides, if I had a tree house, like your mamm wanted us to build, I could always move into it. At least there'd be no oven to burn down the place." He chuckled, as if to lighten the mood.

"Ha! Not funny, Dad."

He winked at her, then pointed to

a bird-feeder on a shelf overhead. "I picked that up at the farmers' market the other day. Looks like a log cabin, don't you think?"

"You're right; it does. And speaking of feeders, it looks like some of those you have out in the yard need to be filled. Would you like me to do it?"

"No, I'll take care of it after we eat." He pushed his dilapidated straw hat a little farther back on his head. "I have lots to get done before my sister gets here."

Avoiding eye contact, Arlene managed a brief nod. Not only was Aunt Verna hard of hearing, but she easily became preoccupied, as well. Arlene hoped between Dad and his sister, they wouldn't burn down the house.

Chapter 4

Eustace whistled as he listened to the birds in the trees overhead. Since he'd spent most of the morning pounding nails as he began work on his tree house, he was surprised the birds were singing at all. The blue jays must have been curious as to who was making all the noise, for they squawked in the branches higher up in the tree. After a while, they flew off, seemingly satisfied with their observations. Eustace had been keeping all the feeders full of food, so most of the birds seemed more interested in eating than being bothered by his noise.

He stopped hammering and sipped on the coffee he'd brought out with him. *What a nice morning. Sure wish I had some help with this.*

Eustace had started this project a week ago, two days after Arlene had brought him a casserole for supper. So far he'd managed to nail a ladder to the tree and get started on the base of the tree house. He hoped to finish the floor before his sister got here, sometime this afternoon. He looked forward to seeing Verna again. It had been some time since her last visit. Since she and her husband, Lester, lived in

Geauga County, which was nearly a two-hour drive by car, he didn't see her very often. With the exception of going to some of the local auctions, Eustace didn't travel much, either. He preferred to stick close to home, where he could putter around and create new things. He felt close to Effie here.

In the spring he'd made several bird feeders out of plastic soda pop bottles. During the summer he had constructed a few wind chimes using old pipe, fishing line, and some CDs he'd received in the mail from an Internet provider trying to drum up business. Like he really needed that! Even Eustace's New Order Amish friend didn't have a computer; although Henry was allowed to have a phone in his house. But after painting the CDs in various shades, the wind chimes had turned out quite colorful.

Eustace was content having a phone in a shack he shared with his closest neighbor. With the exception of a few special things, he'd never had a desire for modern conveniences. But the desires he'd once had were set aside when he joined the church and married Effie forty-seven years ago. He'd had a good life here on this farm, and Eustace appreciated every bit of it — from the large two-story house to the rambling barn where he kept many of his treasures — including his fine-looking horses.

He looked toward the fields. The

edges were ablaze with goldenrod, orange jewel weed, and ragweed — the onset of early autumn colors. Even from where Eustace stood, he could see many butterflies flitting from flower to flower on the unappreciated weeds. Most people he knew didn't care for these intrusive plants, but all three had healing benefits. Even Effie didn't mind seeing them when they bloomed in August and September. She loved everything about nature. Many times she'd picked the goldenrod and would mix them in with late-blooming wildflowers for a centerpiece on the kitchen table.

Eustace shook his head. Everything he saw these days, even the colorful weeds, made him think about Effie.

Halting his thoughts and stepping back to view the mature maple tree he'd chosen to build his tree house in, Eustace mentally checked off the things he'd done so far, in addition to what still needed to be done.

The first phase had been to draw a design of the tree house. Then he'd laid out the wood and all the tools he would need to accomplish his task. Next, Eustace had nailed a ladder to the tree trunk, making it easy to trim the extra branches that could get in the way during construction. He was now in the process of nailing some well-polished wooden boards together across two strong branches, close to each other. This would become the floor of his tree house. Following that, he would add wooden boards on three sides of the tree house until a railing was formed. The door and windows would then be installed for cross-ventilation. A wooden roof would follow, and then it would be time for the finishing touches.

A terrace would be nice, so I can sit out there and feel one with the birds, Eustace mused. *Effie would like it.* He gave a decisive nod. "Jah, that's what I'm gonna do all right."

"Are you talkin' to yourself, Grandpa?"

Eustace turned so abruptly, he nearly fell over backward. "Whoa there, Doug. You shouldn't sneak up on me!"

Eustace's twelve-year-old grandson motioned to his bike. "I wasn't sneakin'. I rode right in. Figured you'd hear me comin'."

Eustace shook his head. "Nope. Never heard a thing. Guess it's because I was concentrating on this." He gestured to the pieces of wood lying on the ground beneath the tree.

Doug's mouth formed an *O*. "Are ya finally gonna make the tree house you've been talkin' about?"

"Jah. I'd say it's about time, too, wouldn't you?"

The boy nodded enthusiastically. "Can I help ya with it?"

"It's more than all right with me, if your mamm doesn't mind. You're an assiduous kid, aren't ya, boy?"

Doug's head titled slightly to the left. "Assiduous?"

"Sorry, never mind." Eustace's brows furrowed. "Say, shouldn't you be in school right now?"

"School's out for the day, Grandpa. I told Mama this morning I was comin' by here afterward. I wanted to spend some time alone with you, without my sisters and little brother taggin' along."

Eustace gave his earlobe a tug. "Guess I've been out here longer than I thought. I didn't even take time to eat anything at noon."

"Want my banana, Grandpa? I've got one in my lunch pail I didn't eat for lunch."

Eustace ruffled the boy's thick

brown hair. "No, that's okay. Your mamm gave it to you, so you'd better eat it."

"She won't mind. Long as I don't come home with it." Doug wrinkled his nose. "Mama gets upset if any of her kinner waste food."

"We wouldn't want your mamm gettin' upset, now would we?" Eustace reached into Doug's lunch pail and withdrew the banana. He was about to peel it when a gray minivan pulled into the yard and parked. Verna stepped out and grabbed her suitcase.

Eustace cupped his hands around his mouth and gave a yell. "We're back here!"

Grinning like a child who'd been given a balloon, Verna set her suitcase down and began walking toward Eustace, sneezing as she came.

He smiled back at her. *So, let the fun begin.*

They waved as her driver turned the van around and pulled out of the driveway. "I'll give a call to my driver a few days before I decide to return home," Verna said. "She'll be staying in Sugarcreek with some friends while she's here, so I don't think she's in a hurry to get home."

When she approached, Verna gave Eustace a sisterly hug. "It's sure good to see you again. It's been awhile, hasn't it?"

Eustace bobbed his head.

Glancing at Doug, Verna asked, "Now who is this handsome young man with you today?"

"This is Doug — Arlene's son."

She looked at him strangely. "Did you say 'Bug'?"

"No, I said the boy's name is Doug." Eustace spoke a little louder, remembering Verna was hard of hearing.

"Well, goodness me. You've sure grown since I last saw you." She held out her arms. "Now Doug, how about a hug for your great-aunt Verna?" Her eyes twinkled with merriment.

Doug snickered, and a bit awkwardly, he complied.

"Just to let you both know, my hearing's not the best these days." Verna's voice rose with each word. "So you may have to repeat what you've said sometimes." Clucking her tongue, she shook her head. "It sure isn't easy gettin' older."

"Let's take you inside and put your things away." Eustace walked to the driveway, where she had left her suitcase and picked it up. "The sheets are clean on the guest bed, and a little tidying's been done. Arlene took care of it when she was here the other day."

"It's nice to be with you, Brother, and to be able to spend time with your family." Verna spoke excitedly. Stepping onto the porch, she stopped and pointed to his boots. "For goodness' sakes, Eustace, those boots of yours are in need of repair. If you're not careful, they'll fall right off your feet." She elbowed him and chuckled. "Maybe you ought to put some duct tape on them. Then they'll match the old hat on your head."

Eustace reached up and touched the spot on the brim of his hat, where duct tape held it together. "You may have a point, Sister. If I repaired the boots I could keep wearin' them longer. Maybe I'll do that while you're getting settled in."

Eustace had no more than finished taping up his boots when Verna came out to the kitchen. "How's this look?" He leaned back in his chair and stuck out his feet.

Covering her mouth with her hand, she giggled like she had when she was a girl. "It might hold them together for a while, but they sure look *schpassich*."

"They may look funny, but they'll serve the purpose." Eustace rolled his chair across the floor and picked up a flyer off his old desk. "Say, Verna, I have an idea of something fun we could do while you're here." He held the paper out to her.

Pushing her glasses a little higher on her nose, she studied the flyer. "So there's going to be an auction up in Mt. Hope tomorrow morning, huh?"

He gave a quick nod. "Would you like to go, or will you be too tired?"

"I'm not tired at all. In fact, it sounds like fun."

Eustace grinned. "Oh, good. Who knows what interesting things we might find to bid on?"

"Guess we'll have to hire a driver since it's not close by."

"Not a problem. I'll go out to the phone shack and make the call right now." Eustace rose from his chair, but paused at the door. "Would ya mind if I invite my friend Henry to come along?"

She shook her head. "Not a'tall."

"Okay, good. I'll make the phone calls now, and then I need to get back to work on my tree house." He put on his straw hat. "Don't want to keep my grandson waitin' for me all day."

"You go right ahead." Verna gave Eustace's arm a tender squeeze. "I'll stay here in the kitchen and see what I can fix for supper."

Eustace smiled and headed out the door. He found Doug sitting on the top porch step with his chin in his hands. "I'm ready to go to work, Grandpa."

"I'll be with you shortly." Eustace tapped the boy's shoulder. "Just need to make a few phone calls, then we can work till it's time for you to go home for supper."

Akron

Today had been Joel's first day back on the job, and even though all he'd done was drive around in his truck to bid on a few jobs, he was beat. The driving hadn't worn him out, though; it was his anxiety over the money he still owed, coupled with the fact he didn't know if any of his bids would even be accepted. Money . . . money . . . money. It seemed the almighty dollar was constantly on his mind. He needed work, and he needed it bad. If something didn't open up soon, he may have to sell one of his vehicles.

"It won't be the Corvette," Joel mumbled after he entered his home and headed for the shower. "If I sell anything, it would be my everyday car, but I need it in case my truck gives out."

Joel stepped into the bathroom and looked in the mirror. He clearly needed a shave, and his eyes were puffy and bloodshot from lack of sleep. *After I get cleaned up maybe I'll take the Vette out for a spin. That should perk me right up.* Since Kristi had said she'd be working the evening shift and wouldn't be coming by like she'd been doing since Joel's accident, he had the perfect opportunity to do whatever he wanted.

Joel ran his fingers through the back of his hair. *Maybe I'll call my buddy Tom and see what he's up to this evening. I'll bet he'll jump at the chance to take another ride in my Corvette.*

When Kristi got off work at ten o'clock that evening, she was tempted to drive by Joel's and check on him. But since today was his first day back on the job, he was probably exhausted and had gone to bed by now. She'd been fixing his supper every night since he got out of the hospital and felt bad she'd been unable to do it for him this evening. Some of the casserole was left over from what she'd fixed him last night. Hopefully Joel had warmed it up for his supper.

Kristi turned on the radio and tried to relax. It seemed like she was always worried about Joel these days. His haggard appearance told her he wasn't sleeping well, and his lack of enthusiasm when they talked most likely meant he was depressed. Either that or he'd become bored with her.

Kristi's confidence in her relationship with Joel often wavered. Things were different from when they'd first started dating.

She gripped the steering wheel as another thought popped into her head. *Could Joel be attracted to someone else? Maybe that's why he isn't opening up to me.*

She turned the radio up, trying to drown out her thoughts, but it was no use. Her concern for Joel was uppermost in her mind — especially when their favorite song began to play. Last night when she'd made supper for him, he'd been moody and had even snapped at her a couple of times. She had tried to ignore it, realizing he was under a lot of stress and probably still sore from his accident, but his sharp tone hurt nonetheless. Even in her worst mood, Kristi had never talked harshly to Joel.

"Lord, please help me with this." She turned off the radio and prayed out loud. "If things are okay between Joel and me, then erase my doubts. If there's a problem and Joel decides we should break up, please help me accept it as Your will and be able to move on with my life."

Tears stung Kristi's eyes. She'd had other boyfriends, but never loved any of them the way she did Joel. She couldn't imagine her life without him. But if they did at some point end up going their separate ways, she would have to deal with it, no matter how much it hurt.

Up ahead, Kristi noticed a nice-looking car parked along the side of the road. When she drew closer, she realized it was Joel and his friend Tom walking from the front of the car as they put the hood back down. *"I wonder what's going on. Joel should be home in bed. At least I thought he would be."*

Joel couldn't believe it when Kristi pulled up alongside of them. He and Tom had been out tooling around for a good many hours until something started sputtering in the engine. They had discovered a disconnected hose and been able to fix it. Fortunately, the engine was running smoothly again.

Joel jammed his hands into his pockets. "Hey, what are you doing here? I thought you'd be in bed by now."

"I'm on my way home from work. I worked the evening shift, remember? I thought you'd be in bed by now, too." Kristi bit her bottom lip. "Do you need some help?"

He smacked his forehead. "I knew you planned to work late. Guess I momentarily forgot." He hesitated then quickly explained, "Tom wanted me to go for a ride and take his new car out for a spin. Guess we didn't realize it was this late."

"Nice car, Tom." Kristi smiled. "It looks expensive."

"Uh . . . yeah, it is." Tom looked at Joel, while responding to Kristi.

Relieved that Tom didn't contradict him, Joel explained about the disconnected hose. He'd sure never expected her to come along.

"I can give you a lift home if you like," Kristi offered.

"Thanks but my truck is back at Tom's. I'll give you a call tomorrow."

Joel watched as Kristi waved and pulled away. He also felt Tom's eyes boring into the back of his head.

"I can't believe you would drag me into your lie." Tom pointed a finger at Joel.

"I plan on telling her about this car. I'm just not sure when."

Joel couldn't blame Tom for being upset with him. One of these days, he'd have a lot of explaining to do, and he hoped Kristi would understand.

CHAPTER 5

Walnut Creek, Ohio

"Hey, Sister, wait up!" Elsie called when she spotted Doris in front of Der Dutchman's Bakery.

Doris halted and turned around. "It's good to see you. Did you come for breakfast?"

Elsie shook her head. "I'm heading to Charm to see Dad this morning and thought I'd stop by the bakery first to pick up some of his favorite lemon fry pies. I also want to see if Aunt Verna is here yet. She was supposed to arrive at Dad's sometime yesterday, and this evening I want to have everyone for supper at my house. Can you come?"

Doris nodded. "Jah, I heard she was coming, and so far, we're free for supper tonight. How long will Aunt Verna be visiting?"

"Probably a week or two. I'm sure Dad's going to enjoy her company. Even though he insists he's getting along fine on his own, Dad's bound to get lonely living there all alone."

"You're right, but I doubt any of us will ever convince him to move into one of our homes." Doris frowned. "You know Dad. He can be so stubborn sometimes."

"I can't argue with that." Elsie

touched her sister's arm. "How are you and Brian these days? Are you both working hard at your jobs?"

"Jah. In fact, I need to get going right now, or I'll be late for work. I'm doing the breakfast and lunch shifts today."

"Then I guess you'll be busy with all the fall tourists."

Doris moved her head slowly up and down. "Sometimes I wish I could quit waitressing and stay home." She lifted her shoulders in a brief shrug. "But then what would I do all day with no *kinner* to take care of?"

Elsie gave Doris a hug. "Maybe you and Brian should consider adopting a *boppli.*"

Tears pooled in Doris's eyes. "I'd

like to, but Brian says if God wants us to have a baby, it will happen in His time. He won't even talk about adoption."

Elsie wanted to say more, but she didn't want to upset Doris further or cause her to be late for work. "Always remember, I've been praying for you and will continue to do so."

"Danki. That means a lot." Doris took a tissue from her purse and dried her eyes. "I'd better get going. Unless you hear differently, Brian and I will join you for supper. Oh, and before I forget, can I bring anything to add to the meal?"

"All you need to bring are your hearty appetites." Elsie grinned.

As Doris walked away, Elsie

paused. *Heavenly Father, if Doris is never going to have any children of her own, please soften Brian's heart on the subject of adoption.*

Sighing, she headed for the bakery. As soon as she stepped inside, her senses were greeted by the sweet aroma of cookies and pastries. The place was already busy with tourists looking around and trying some samples. Elsie walked by the bakery cases to check out what might interest her. The lemon fry pies looked good. But so did the frosted lemon cookies. Most anything lemon Dad would like. *Maybe I'll get some of each,* she decided. *Dad can take home whatever we don't eat for supper tonight. That way he and Aunt Verna can snack on them later this week.*

As she stood in line, waiting to pay for her things, Elsie noticed an English woman and a young girl ahead of her. The girl had turned to face Elsie and kept staring at her, even though the child's mother told her several times to turn around. When the woman finished paying, she turned to Elsie and cleared her throat. "I apologize for my daughter's behavior. This is our first trip to Amish country, and she's curious about the clothes you're wearing."

"It's okay. I understand." This was not the first time Elsie had caught someone staring at her. What she didn't appreciate was when they took photos without her permission. While some Amish might not care too much, the district she belonged to frowned on having their pictures taken.

After Elsie paid for the cookies and fry pies, she went outside to her buggy and put her things up front. She'd also picked up an éclair to nibble on during her journey. After she untied her horse and climbed in the buggy, she grabbed the bakery bag and took out the tasty treat. Now she was ready to stop by Dad's for a quick visit and to invite him and Aunt Verna for supper tonight.

Charm

"How'd ya sleep last night?" Eustace asked his sister as they sat at his kitchen table eating breakfast.

"Other than my sneezing spell, I slept just fine. Can't think of any reason I wouldn't have, though. It's nice and *friedlich* here."

"I can't argue with you; it is peaceful." Eustace reached for the ketchup and squirted some on his scrambled eggs, as well as the hash browns Verna had made. "What got ya to sneezing all of a sudden?"

"I must be allergic to the goldenrod. It's blooming at home as well." Verna wiped her nose with a tissue, then went to the sink to wash her hands. "I'd planned on going to the doctor to see if he could give me something, but haven't gotten there yet." She sat down again.

"It's most likely the ragweed making you sneeze," Eustace explained. "Although goldenrod is often blamed during allergy season, it doesn't have airborne pollen and doesn't cause allergic reactions like ragweed does."

"You learn something new every day." Verna smiled, looking at Eustace over her glasses.

"I read recently that goldenrod's pollen is stickier, and instead of it blowing in the wind, it's spread by the butterflies, ants, and bees."

"That's interesting. Sure hope I'm not sneezing the whole time I'm here." Verna spread some jelly on her piece of toast. "It seems to come in spurts."

"Are you ready to go to the auction today? Maybe you'll feel better there — at least for a while."

She tipped her head. "What did you say?"

Speaking a little louder this time, Eustace repeated his question.

"*Jah*. I'm looking forward to it." She drank some orange juice. "Will you be looking for anything in particular?"

"Nothing special. Sometimes I don't know what I want till I see it."

Verna chuckled. "I'm the same way whenever I go shopping. Makes Lester a nervous wreck, which is why he doesn't go with me too often."

Eustace sighed. "Effie used to go to auctions with me. It was her time to socialize while I bid on whatever things caught my fancy. I'll never forget the look on her face when I carried a box of old cowboy boots out to the buggy one day."

"What were you planning to do with them?"

"Didn't really know at the time, but I ended up planting some flowers in them." Eustace grinned. "Afterward, Effie kind of liked them."

Verna smiled. "I'll bet you still miss her a lot."

"Jah. There isn't a day that goes by I don't think about my *fraa.*" Eustace glanced out the window at the line of trees behind his house. "The tree house I'm building is in memory of Effie."

Verna's eyes widened. "How nice!

I did notice you were working on something when I arrived yesterday afternoon, but I was so excited to be here, I didn't pay much attention to what you'd been doing. How far have you gotten on it?"

"Not much — just built the platform so far. My grandson Doug wants to come help again, and his little *bruder* Scott will probably do whatever he can as well. Course, he's only eight years old, so he'll mostly be handing us whatever tools we need. He can be our little gofer."

"If my seventy-five-year-old body could still move like it once did, I'd be right in there, helping you build the tree house."

Eustace grunted. "My sixty-five-year-old body doesn't move as it once did, either, but I figure as long as I keep using my limbs, they're less apt to stop workin' for me." He winked at her. "You've heard the old saying 'Use it or lose it.' "

"You're absolutely right. It's best to keep moving." Verna pushed away from the table. "As soon as I get the *gscharr* done, I'd like to see where you're building the tree house."

"Sounds good to me. Only, let's leave the dishes and go look at it now."

Verna didn't have to be asked twice. Like Eustace, she'd always been eager to try new things and was a spur-of-the-moment kind of person. Eventually, the dishes would get done, but they could soak in the sink until they got back to the house.

Slipping into her black sweater and putting a tissue inside her sleeve, Verna headed out the door with Eustace right behind.

When Elsie pulled her horse up to Dad's hitching rail, she heard voices in the distance. Apparently Dad and Aunt Verna were somewhere outside.

After securing the horse, Elsie stood and listened a few seconds. Then, realizing the voices came from the trees out back, she headed in that direction. *I'll bet Dad's showing Aunt Verna where he plans to build his tree house.*

As Elsie approached the spot, her mouth dropped open. In the week since she'd been here, Dad had built a platform in the tree that once held his suspenders captive. But the work he'd accomplished in such a short time wasn't what surprised her the most. The real shock was seeing both Dad and his sister sitting on the platform.

"Wie geht's?" Aunt Verna called down to Elsie. "It's good to see you again."

"I'm doing fine, and apparently so are you." She tipped her head back, shielding her eyes from the glare of the sun peeking through the tree branches. "I never expected to see you and Dad up there."

"What was it you said?" Aunt

Verna leaned her head forward.

"I never expected to see you and Dad up there." Elsie repeated, a little louder this time.

"You never know what we old retired people will do." Aunt Verna grinned. "Or maybe I should have said, 'What we tired old people will do.'"

"I brought her out to see what I've accomplished so far," Dad explained. "And she got the bright idea to climb up the ladder to admire the view."

"That's right." Aunt Verna bobbed her head. "Your daed was trying to describe to me what he wants for this tree house. Maybe a little porch on the front or back and some windows with good views. I can't wait to see the finished project." She stood and rubbed her back. "And what a view it is from here. Why, I can see clear back on your daed's property where the oil wells are located."

Elsie frowned. She'd never mentioned anything to Dad, but she was none too happy about those oil well monstrosities. They'd given Dad more money than he knew what to do with, but money didn't bring true happiness. Truth was, Dad hadn't been happy since Joel left home. Mama dying a few years ago had only added to his despair.

"Why don't you come on up?" Aunt Verna called. "There's room for three of us up here."

"No thanks." Elsie shook her

head. "I just stopped by to drop off some cookies and lemon fry pies and see if you two would like to join the rest of the family for supper at my house tonight. Maybe Dad could bring his harmonica along and play some music for us after we eat."

"Sounds good to me," Verna shouted.

"We'll be leaving for the auction soon, but should be back in plenty of time," Dad added.

"I hope I get to see Joel while I'm here. Is your bruder coming tonight?"

"No, he will not be joining the family," Dad answered before Elsie could respond. "Joel doesn't want anything to do with us. But I will bring my harmonica tonight."

Aunt Verna stared down at Elsie, who couldn't help wondering what Dad's sister was thinking. Did she realize how bitter Dad felt about Joel? *If I did invite Joel to supper, would he come?*

CHAPTER 6

Akron

Not more than two minutes after Joel left a job in Canton, his cell phone rang. Since he hadn't started the truck yet, he answered the call.

"Hi, Joel. It's Elsie. Are you busy right now?"

"Uh, no. I'm done working for the day and am getting ready to head home." He rolled down his window to get some air flowing.

"I won't keep you, but I wanted to tell you Aunt Verna came down

119

from Burton to spend some time with Dad. We're all having supper at our house this evening, and I was wondering if you'd like to join us." Elsie paused. "I'm sure Aunt Verna would love to see you."

Yeah, well, she'd probably be the only one. Joel drew in a sharp breath. He had fond memories of his aunt, but Dad would be there. After their last confrontation, Joel wasn't about to put himself in a similar situation. Most likely, Dad would give him the cold shoulder all evening, or they could end up having angry words again.

"Sorry, Elsie, but I can't make it tonight," Joel responded. "Would you tell Aunt Verna hello for me?"

"Of course I will, but I'm sorry

you won't be able to join us."

"Yeah, me too."

"Guess I'd better let you go."

"Okay. Thanks for calling. Bye, Elsie." Joel grabbed his bottle of water from the cooler on the floor and took a drink. It was good to get in some work today. Tomorrow looked promising as well. Putting his water in the cup holder, he realized his cell phone was still in his grasp. After he put it away, he sat in his truck for a while, staring out the front window. He was glad his sister hadn't pressed him further when he'd declined her invitation. Sometimes Joel felt like a buggy without a horse, no longer being close to his family. But it was a choice he'd made. He only wished he felt free to visit without harsh words between him and Dad. Deep down, Joel figured there might come a day when he'd regret all this. He wouldn't have the memories his sisters had of family events, get-togethers around the holidays, and other fun times. If only his family would be more accepting of the choice he'd made for his life. Didn't he deserve to be happy, too? If they had accepted his choices — especially Dad — maybe he'd feel more comfortable around them.

Of course, Joel reasoned, *it's partly my fault because I asked him for money.* He tapped his knuckles against the steering wheel, wishing once more his father wasn't so stingy.

"Dad didn't even give me a chance. I would have paid it back," he muttered. "Just like I'll return the money to Kristi's and my bank account. It's going to take a little time, that's all."

Walnut Creek

"So what did you and Grandpa do today?" Elsie's oldest son, Glen, asked, smiling at Verna from across the dining-room table.

She leaned slightly forward, cupping her hand around her ear. "Sorry, I didn't hear what you said."

Glen repeated his question, while Eustace waited to see if his sister would respond. If she still didn't get what Glen said, Eustace was prepared to answer for her.

"We spent some time looking at his tree house. Then we went to an auction with his friend Henry." Verna smiled as her gaze touched each person gathered around Elsie's table.

"It's so nice to be here with all of you this evening. The whole family is here tonight — everyone except Joel."

Eustace curled his toes. He was tempted to blurt out about Joel never coming around unless he wanted something but thought better of it. This wasn't a topic to be discussed in front of the children.

Why couldn't my son be a part of this family? Eustace asked himself. *Doesn't he realize how much he's missing? Of course, he probably wasn't told about our family gathering in honor of Verna being here. Even if he had known, I'm sure he wouldn't have come.*

Quickly redirecting his thoughts, lest he give in to negativity, Eustace announced he'd brought his harmonica along and would accompany Verna on her autoharp after the meal.

Elsie's daughters, Mary and Hope, clapped their hands, which brought a round of applause from everyone else.

"We can listen to the music and sing all night," enthused Lillian, Arlene's eleven-year-old daughter.

Lillian's father, Larry, tweaked her nose. "We can stay for a little while after supper, but it won't be late. You have school tomorrow, remember?"

"Jah, I know." Lillian looked over at Verna. "Would ya teach me how to play the autoharp?"

Verna grinned, after wiping her nose on a tissue. "I don't see why not. I was about your age when I learned, so I bet you'll catch on mighty fast."

Lillian's eyes brightened even more. "Oh, good. I can hardly wait!"

"Do ya have a cold?" Eighteen-year-old Blaine looked intently at Verna.

"No, it's only my allergies kicking up from the ragweed pollen in the air right now."

Eustace nodded his head as Verna glanced over at him and winked. She'd been paying attention earlier when he'd explained the difference between ragweed and goldenrod.

Scott turned to Eustace and clasped his arm. "Think I could learn how to play the mouth harp, Grandpa?"

"I believe so." Eustace remembered back to the days when his father had taught him to play the harmonica. "It's easy, my boy. Like my daed taught me, all you have to do is suck and blow."

A knot formed in Eustace's stomach as he thought about the day he'd told Joel those same words. Joel had caught on right away and was soon able to play nearly as well as Eustace. What a joy it had been whenever the two of them played duets, with Effie and Joel's three sisters singing along. Those days were gone for him and Joel, but at least Eustace could enjoy the camaraderie of his grandchildren. He felt grateful for the new memories being made.

He reached for his glass of buttermilk and took a drink. *I wonder if Joel will ever have any children of his own.*

Akron

Joel didn't feel much like eating, so he grabbed a cup of coffee, along with his harmonica, and went outside. Fall-like breezes piggy-backed on what was still left of summer —

a perfect evening to enjoy the out-
doors. Autumn was only one week
away, and Joel couldn't help antici-
pating what it would bring. He was
definitely ready for it, especially
with his type of job. Working in the
construction business brought in
good money when he had work to
do and the jobs were big enough.
It had its downside, though —
especially during the sweltering
summers and bitter cold winter
months. Some days were so hot, he
and his subcontractors had to start
work before the sun came up and
stop before the hottest part of the
day. In the winter, it could get so
cold at times that he couldn't feel
his fingers, even with work gloves
on. With those extreme tempera-

tures, Joel felt he really earned his pay. He just wished spring and autumn, with their more moderate temperatures, would last longer.

A niggle of guilt hit him, knowing he still owed money to the guys who worked hard for him. Plus, he needed to get the money back into the joint savings account.

Taking a seat at the picnic table, Joel lifted the harmonica to his lips and began to play a familiar tune — one his dad had taught him when he was a boy.

The longer Joel played, the more he thought about the past — days when everything seemed so much simpler. Soon, the calmness he'd first felt when he came outside was replaced with anxiety. He and Dad used to do many things together when Joel was a boy, but they'd drifted apart during Joel's teenage years. From there, things went downhill quickly, and when Joel left the Amish faith, his close relationship with Dad ended.

"I've got to stop thinking about the past." Joel put the harmonica in his pocket and headed for his shop to look at the Corvette. "I'm not going to get all sentimental about this. It is what it is." If he sat in the comfortable car seat for a while, he might feel better. Maybe he'd take the Vette out for a spin. Driving around on the open road had helped the last time he'd done it — that is until Kristi showed up. He'd felt so humiliated dragging his friend Tom into a lie and had endured even more shame by being dishonest with Kristi. Yet he still didn't have the nerve to tell her the truth.

When Joel entered his shop, he paused and looked around. The building was huge — more than enough room to house all his tools, plus several classic cars. Of course, at the rate things were going, it didn't look like Joel would own any more than the one he had now. Classics — especially the kind he was after — cost a lot of money.

"Guess it's just wishful thinking," Joel mumbled. He was about to take a seat inside the car when he heard what sounded like Kristi's car pull into his yard. Joel jumped out of the car, covered it with a tarp, and left the shop, closing and locking the door behind him. He was surprised to see her because she hadn't mentioned anything about coming over.

Smiling, Kristi walked over to Joel. "You look surprised. Aren't you happy to see me?"

"Of course I am." Joel pulled her close and gave her a hug. "I didn't realize you were coming. Didn't you say something about going to the gym to work out tonight?"

"That was my original plan, but I jogged after I got off work so I didn't think I needed any more exercise." Kristi reached for his hand. "What's in your shirt pocket, Joel? Is it your harmonica?"

"Yep, it's my harmonica. I played it awhile before you got here." He stifled a yawn.

"Would you play something for me?" Her eyes lit up. "I haven't heard you play in a long while."

"Okay." Joel placed the harmonica between his lips.

Kristi seemed to enjoy his song. Soon, she started clapping and singing along.

"How about we take a break now?" Joel paused after several songs. "I've had a long, busy day, and I'm tired."

"No problem. Maybe someday you'll teach our child to play." She looked at him sincerely.

"Yeah, if we ever have any kids. To tell you the truth, I'm not sure

I'm cut out to be a father."

Kristi's forehead wrinkled. "You've never mentioned not wanting children before. I've always thought . . ." She dropped her gaze as her voice trailed off.

"Didn't say I don't want any." Joel shrugged his shoulders. "I'm not sure I have what it takes to be a good dad."

Looking up at him again, Kristi squeezed his hand. "Of course you do. You're kind, smart, talented, and a hard worker." She ruffled his hair. "You'll make a great father."

Joel thought about his own father and how he used to think the world of him. Since Joel was no longer a child, he saw Dad for what he was — eccentric, stingy, and unfeeling.

A good father who loves his children would not look the other way when his son has a need.

"Oh, Joel, there's something else I wanted to talk to you about." Kristi's voice halted Joel's thoughts.

Joel led the way to the picnic table and gestured for her to take a seat on the bench. "What's up?"

"As I'm sure you've heard, our church is sponsoring a marriage retreat next week."

"Guess I did read something about it in last Sunday's bulletin."

Nodding, she smiled. "How would you like to go?"

"To the seminar?" His jaw clenched. Seminars or spiritual retreats were not for him.

"Yes."

"Why would we need that? We're not married yet, Kristi."

"It's not only for married couples. It's also for people who are planning to be married."

"Oh, I see."

Kristi's forehead wrinkled. "We are still planning to be married, aren't we? Or have you changed your mind about us?"

Joel shook his head. "Where did you get such an idea? Of course I haven't changed my mind. Now's not a good time to be making any plans."

"I realize that, but if we go to the marriage seminar it might help strengthen our relationship."

He crossed his arms. "What's wrong with our relationship?"

"I . . . I can't put my finger on it, Joel," She paused and swallowed. "Things have been strained between us for a good many weeks. Even before your accident, I felt it."

Joel's chest tightened when he saw tears forming in her eyes. He slid over on the bench and pulled her into his arms. "Sorry, Kristi. I've had a lot on my mind." Kristi felt so warm in his arms; he never wanted to let her go. Joel closed his eyes and held her even tighter. *I'd never be happy if something happened between us.*

"I . . . I know you've been busy."

He gently patted her back, then slowly pulled away, gazing deeply into her ocean-blue eyes. Joel's body flooded with warmth. He could almost feel himself drowning in the depths of her eyes as he gently caressed her cheek. "If it'll make you feel better, I'll go to the marriage conference."

"Thank you, Joel." Kristi sniffed and dabbed at the tears on her cheeks. "I'm confident this will be a good thing for both of us."

He nodded, softly brushing a strand of hair away from her face. Joel wasn't so sure about going to the event, although he wouldn't admit it to her. He didn't need some so-called expert on marriage telling him how to be a good husband. Maybe between now and then he'd get a few more jobs lined up and would be too busy to go.

CHAPTER 7

Kristi pulled up to her parents' house, turned off the engine, and checked her watch. She thought about how she and Joel sat under the stars together last week. It had been wonderful to hear him play the harmonica. It was so nice to see Joel having a good time and looking so relaxed.

Tonight, Kristi and Joel would attend the marriage seminar, and she didn't want to be late. But Mom had called and asked her to stop by. Even though it was Kristi's day off, her Saturday schedule was filling up.

Entering the house, she found her father in the living room, watching TV. "Hey, Dad. How's your back doing?" Kristi bent down and gave him a hug.

"It's better, but the doctor reminded me about taking it easy so I don't reinjure it."

"You should listen to his advice. In the end, you'll be happy you did. It's important to take good care of yourself, because —"

He gestured toward the kitchen and grinned. "Your mother's in there, doing one of her domestic things."

"Okay, Dad, I can take a hint."

Kristi smiled. "Guess I'll go join her."

Placing her purse on a chair, Kristi entered the kitchen and spotted her mother lifting a quart jar from the canner. "Looks like you've been busy."

Mom placed the jar on the counter, then gave Kristi a hug. "I've been making applesauce all morning and thought you might like to take some home." She pointed. "I did all those at the far end earlier, so you can take from them if you like, because those have already cooled."

Kristi studied the jars lined up in a row. The lids on the more recent ones started popping as they cooled.

"I always like to hear that sound." Mom wiped her hands on her apron. "Then I know the lids have sealed."

"They look good, Mom. I'd be happy to take a few jars home." Kristi hoped to do things like this when she and Joel got married. She looked forward to canning and freezing produce from a garden and having fruit trees someday, but recently, some things she'd been wishing for seemed to be getting further out of reach. Kristi almost hated to wish for things, for fear they'd never happen. More than anything, she wanted to become Joel's wife. Lately, though, something felt different between them. Kristi hoped she was wrong about the inner voice, warning her to be on guard. She wanted to trust Joel; after all, along with love, trust was the basis of any relationship.

"I got the applesauce recipe from the Amish cookbook I picked up when you and I visited Holmes County last month." Mom glanced over at Kristi and snapped her fingers. "Hey, are you daydreaming? Didn't you hear what I said?"

"Sorry, Mom. Guess I was zoning out for a bit. I did hear you, though."

Kristi traced the rim of one jar with her finger. "Our trip to Holmes County was a fun weekend. I only wish I'd had enough money to buy a quilt."

Mom gave a nod. "We did see a

lot of beautiful quilts. It's too bad they're so expensive."

"It's understandable, though. A lot of work goes into making one."

"It certainly does." Mom opened the refrigerator and removed a jug of apple cider. "Boy, I'm glad it's autumn now. The cooler temperatures make doing this canning a whole lot easier."

"I'm with you, Mom. I love running when the air is cool and crisp and there aren't a lot of bugs swarming around my head."

"Would you like something cold to drink?"

Kristi smiled. "Maybe half a glass, and then I need to get going."

"What's the rush?"

"Joel and I are going to the marriage seminar our church is hosting this evening. Besides, I have a few things I need to get done at home before it's time to go."

Mom handed Kristi a glass of cider. "Your dad and I thought about going to the seminar, too. Events like this are beneficial, even for people who have been married a long time. All couples need a reminder of the things they need to do to keep their marriage healthy."

"I suppose that's true." Kristi took a drink, allowing the tangy cider to roll around on her tongue before swallowing. One of the best things about fall was enjoying the mouthwatering apples coming into season. "I'm certainly looking forward to going tonight. I hope the things we learn will strengthen Joel's and my relationship." She sighed. "Things have been a bit strained between us lately."

Kristi waited for Mom's response, expecting a reminder of what the Bible says about being unequally yoked. To her surprise, Mom merely patted Kristi's arm and said, "I'm sorry, Kristi. I hope things will go better for you soon."

Nodding, Kristi finished her cider and set the glass in the sink, filling it with warm water to soak. "I'd better get going or I won't get any of the things done on my list today." She gave Mom a hug and started for the back door.

"Don't forget your jars of apple-sauce." Mom put six jars in a cardboard box and handed it to Kristi. "If your dad and I decide to go, we'll see you at the seminar this evening."

"Sounds good." Kristi headed out the door. She'd barely gotten into her car when her cell phone rang. The caller ID spelled out it was Joel.

"Hey, Joel, I was just thinking of you. I'm looking forward to our evening together."

"Umm . . . about that . . . I'm sorry to have to tell you this, but the job I started yesterday isn't done. I'm here right now at the job site, working on it again."

"What time will you get done?"

"I'm not sure — probably not till quite late."

"Can't you finish it on Monday?"

"Nope. It's a rush job and needs to be finished today. So I won't be able to attend the marriage seminar with you tonight after all."

"Oh, I see." Kristi couldn't hide her disappointment. But Joel needed the work, so she would try to be understanding. "Guess I'll go without you then. Maybe I'll get some helpful hints about being a good wife."

"Sorry, Kristi. I feel bad about letting you down."

"No, it's okay. Sometimes work needs to come first. If you're free after church tomorrow, maybe we can have lunch and I'll share with you what I learned."

"Okay, sounds good. See you

tomorrow, Kristi."

Kristi hung up, leaned her head back, and closed her eyes. *I hope Joel really does have to work tonight and isn't using it as an excuse to get out of going to the seminar.* She opened her eyes and started the car. *I'm sure he wouldn't lie to me.*

Charm

When Doris arrived at her dad's place later in the afternoon, she was surprised to find him outside working on the tree house, along with her nephews Scott and Doug, as well as Eustace's friend Henry.

"I see you have quite a crew working here today." Doris walked around some of the boards as she stepped up to the maple Dad had chosen for his tree house.

Dad removed his hat and fanned his face. "Jah, and they're all good helpers." He smiled at Doris. "Did you come to help, too?"

She shook her head. "I heard Aunt Verna will be heading back to Burton this evening, so I came to say goodbye."

"That's right. She's inside doing a little cleaning she insisted needed to be done before she leaves." Dad's forehead wrinkled. "I told her not to bother, but she was adamant."

"Yoo-hoo!" Aunt Verna opened the door and waved. "I saw you pull in, Doris. I've got something I need to show you from the auction the other day." She ambled toward them with a bird cage swaying by her side. It looked old and ornate. A blur of red flapped inside it, too.

Doris couldn't believe her eyes when she recognized the blur as a beautiful red cardinal. The poor thing looked confused. No matter how pretty the cage was, the wild bird would be miserable enduring its sentence. Besides, it wasn't a pet.

"How do you like my new bird cage and its occupant?" Aunt Verna spoke rapidly, her eyes dancing with joy.

Dad cleared his throat. "She's a little proud of her purchase, I'd say." He took over the conversation. "Did you notice my home-made table over there? The base is a wooden wire spool I picked up at the auction. When we got it home, I put a top on it. Not too shabby of a picnic table, either. Henry's coffee cup is setting on it already."

Henry nodded enthusiastically. "It was fun going to the auction with you and Verna. And with all the walking we did, we sure got our exercise, didn't we?" He leaned down and rubbed the calf of his leg. "But it was worth it, because I left there with a few things myself." Using a hanky he took from his pocket, he wiped his brow.

Doris turned to Aunt Verna. "What I'm wondering is how you ended up with our state bird in your birdcage?"

Aunt Verna cupped her hand over

her ear. "What was that?"

Doris repeated her question.

"Oh, well, it was stuck inside one of your daed's bird feeders, so I rescued it. Of course, I cleaned out the bird cage first, then added food and water before I saved the critter from its cramped quarters and heat exhaustion. It was a hot day when I discovered it there."

"But Aunt Verna, the cardinal looks okay now. Wouldn't he be happier if you released him instead?"

Scott and Doug stepped over right then. "The poor bird looks sad." Doug scrunched up his nose. "It ain't fair. You oughta let him go."

"You're probably right. Guess it

would be better to let him fly free like the other birds here in the yard." She unlatched the cage door. "Okay everyone, I'm letting the cardinal go."

All eyes watched in anticipation to see what would happen next. Aunt Verna opened the cage door. The cardinal sat for a moment; then it hopped out and flew away. Dad, Henry, and Aunt Verna smiled. The boys clapped. Doris felt relief. She couldn't believe anyone would try to make a pet out of a wild bird. But then, like Dad, Aunt Verna had a good many eccentricities.

"How's your mare doing with the new foal?" Doris asked, turning to Dad.

"They're both doing well."

"Wanna go out to the barn and take a look?" Scott tugged on Doris's arm.

She smiled and took his hand. "I'd like that. Lead the way."

"I'll walk with you. I need a break from housecleaning." Aunt Verna set the empty bird cage on the ground.

"After we see the horse, I'll be happy to help you finish cleaning Dad's house," Doris offered.

Aunt Verna slipped her arm around Doris's waist and chatted as the three of them made their way to the barn.

When they returned from the barn, Doris noticed Henry crouched near a metal bucket with nails scattered on the ground. She knelt beside him and offered to help pick them up.

"That's nice of you." He grimaced. "Guess I'd better pay closer attention to what I'm doing. I'm gettin' clumsy in my old age."

"Everyone drops things from time to time, Henry." Doris patted his arm. "It's good of you to help Dad with his new project."

"That's why Grandpa's tree house is goin' up so fast." Scott pointed overhead. "He's got plenty of help to get the job done."

Doris smiled. "I'm sure he appreciates each of you being here today."

Aunt Verna nodded. "I bet, too."

Scott grinned up at Doris. "I can't wait till the tree house is done and we can all go up in it."

Doris squeezed his shoulder. "You can count me out. I've never liked heights."

"What about Uncle Joel? Does he like bein' up high?"

"He used to," Dad answered before Doris could respond. "Joel was like a monkey when it came to climbing trees."

Scott's eyes lit up. "Wish I'd known him when he was a *bu.*"

"You'd have gotten along well, I'm sure."

"You're probably right." Doug nodded. "My little bruder gets along with everyone. Course, he can be kinda stubborn sometimes, and he —"

"I wish Uncle Joel was here workin' on the tree house with us," Scott interrupted.

"We have plenty of help." Dad motioned to Henry. "My good friend came to work on the tree house."

"Yep." Henry's eyes twinkled. "Even my dog, Peaches, wanted to come along." He winked at Scott. "She's not afraid of heights, either."

"You mean she'll climb the ladder up to the tree house?" Doug questioned.

"That's right." Henry chuckled. "When it comes to climbing, my *hund's* like a mountain goat."

The boys laughed, along with Aunt Verna. Doris rolled her eyes.

"Henry you're such a tease."

He wiggled his silver-gray brows. "Wasn't teasing. If I climbed a ladder, or even a tree, Peaches would come right up after me. Wanna see?"

"I do! I do!" Scott bounced up and down on his toes. "I've never seen a dog climb a ladder before."

"And you're not gonna see one today, either." Dad gestured to the pile of wood on the ground. "We're supposed to be working, not foolin' around."

"I'll tell ya what, son." Henry bent over to stroke Peaches on the head. "When the tree house is finished, I'll let Peaches climb up to the top."

"Okay." Scott looked toward the

house. "Is it all right if I go get a drink?"

"Course you can. While you're in there, would ya bring the rest of us some bottles of water?"

"Sure, Grandpa." Scott headed for the house. Doris and Aunt Verna followed.

When they stepped inside, Scott paused and turned to her. "Have ya seen Uncle Joel lately, Aunt Doris?"

"No. Why would I?" she asked, a bit too sharply.

"Thought maybe he's come in to eat at the restaurant where you work."

Doris shook her head. "If he has, it's been on the days I haven't worked."

"I liked being with Uncle Joel the last time he visited. Sure wish he'd come around more often."

Doris nodded. "We'd all like that, Scott, but it's probably not going to happen."

"How come?"

"My bruder is a busy contractor. He doesn't have much free time." Doris could have told him a lot more, but thought better of it. Scott was too young to understand everything concerning Joel. She would not be guilty of talking badly about him.

CHAPTER 8

Yipe! Yipe! Yipe!

Eustace turned to Scott and shook his finger. "You'd better be prudent with what you're doin' now, 'cause ya stepped on the dog's tail."

The boy jumped back. "Oops! Sorry about that. Didn't realize she was sittin' behind me."

"It's okay." Henry bent down and picked up his dog. "Peaches has a way of getting underfoot." He stroked her tail. "She'll be fine.

Probably scared her more than any-thing."

"Would it be all right if I hold her?" Doug questioned.

"Don't see why not." Henry handed the pooch to Doug and stood watching as Peaches licked the boy's nose. In no time, Peaches grew limp in Doug's arms. Her big brown eyes drifted lazily closed as the boy twirled his fingers around her cottony curls.

It was time to get back to work, so Eustace climbed the ladder to the floor of his tree house. He picked up his hammer to begin working on the next phase of the project — the railing and deck, when he heard Doug mention Anna Detweiler's name.

"Ya know what, Henry? My teacher let the scholars bring their pets to school last Friday."

"Is that so?" Henry leaned against the ladder, as if he was in no mood to work.

"Jah, but the only pet I have is my pony, Flicker, and my folks wouldn't let me take her to school." Doug's voice lowered a bit, and Eustace had to strain to hear what he said next. "Sure wish I had a hund like Peaches. She's real nice."

"You and me think alike," Henry agreed. "If she wasn't around, things wouldn't be the same."

"Teacher Anna has a cocker spaniel, too, only hers is all black. When she brought the dog on pet day, everyone in the class got to pet it."

"Anna sounds like a nice teacher."

She would have been a nice daughter-in-law, too, Eustace thought. *But wishing for what could have been won't change the facts. Joel left a girl everyone believed he would marry, and now he probably doesn't even give her a thought.*

"Say, Henry. Are you gonna stand there all day watchin' the dog, or did you plan on helping me build the tree house?" Eustace called down to his friend.

Henry tipped his head back and looked up. "I'm old. Leave me alone."

"And I'm not?" Eustace laughed so hard, tears ran down his cheeks. He figured he and Henry could probably outwork his two grandsons put together.

"I'll help ya, Grandpa." Scott scampered up the ladder. "Tell me what you want done, and I'll do it."

"You can start by handing me a few of those." Eustace pointed to a can of nails. "We can only work another hour, and then it'll be time for you boys to go home for supper."

"Sure, Grandpa, whatever you say."

Eustace was pleased at the young boy's eagerness to help. Joel had been the same way when he was Scott's age — always helpful and eager to please. Why couldn't things have stayed the way they were back then?

Holding a board in place, Eustace

clenched the hammer and drove a nail in so hard, his hand ached. *I need to stop thinking about Joel and concentrate on the joy of building this special tree house in memory of Effie.* Looking down at Henry and Doug, Eustace cupped his hands around his mouth and hollered, "We could sure use more help up here! Could one of you bring me another batch of boards?"

"I'll do it! Can't let my little bruder do all the work." Doug handed Peaches back to Henry, grabbed some boards, and climbed up the ladder.

Eustace smiled. He hoped these two boys would grow into strong men who followed the Lord's leading in all they said and did. If they put God first, He would lead and guide them through all of their days.

Eustace closed his eyes briefly and sent up a prayer. *It's what I want for my son, too, Lord. I pray the decision I made awhile back about Joel and the rest of my kinner was the right thing to do.*

"It's been nice visiting with you, but now it's time for me to head home. Brian will be there soon, and I need to get supper started." Doris gave her aunt a hug, then turned toward the door. "I hope we will get to see you again soon."

"What was it you just said?" Aunt Verna asked.

Doris turned back around. "I'm

sorry, Aunt Verna. I said, 'I hope we get to see you again soon.' "

"No harm done. The ole' hearing isn't what it used to be." Aunt Verna smiled. "Maybe the next time I come, my husband will join me."

"That would be nice. I haven't seen Uncle Lester in some time."

"He doesn't travel as much as he used to, with his arthritis and all."

"I understand." Doris gave Aunt Verna another hug. "What time will your driver be here to pick you up?"

"She's supposed to come around seven. It will give your daed and me time to have supper and say our goodbyes." Aunt Verna walked with Doris out to the porch. "Maybe next time I come, Joel will be here.

It would have been nice to have seen him this time."

A lump formed in Doris's throat. She swallowed hard and gave a brief nod. At this point, the chance of Uncle Lester leaving Burton to travel anywhere was greater than Joel coming here — unless he wanted something.

Doris went out and told everyone goodbye, then headed for the barn to get her horse. As she walked the mare out to hook her up, Doris couldn't wait to share with Brian about her day. She would make homemade pizza and a tossed salad. Then she and Brian could sit down to a quiet meal and visit. She thought it strange how the English liked to watch TV. Even some restaurants would have it on. Doris was thankful TVs held no place in an Amish home. It would only be a distraction. And from what she'd heard, some things shown on the television could lead a person astray.

A yawn escaped her lips as she climbed into the buggy and gathered up the reins. It had been busy at Dad's today, but she and Aunt Verna had gotten a lot done. Doris would miss her father's sister. It felt nice to have a mother-figure around.

After guiding her horse onto the main road, Doris relaxed in her seat, pleased there wasn't much traffic. The fall scenery was beautiful, too — so many leaves already turning color. It was enough to melt away her cares.

With the sun beginning to set over the hills, it was almost time to send the boys home. Eustace didn't want them riding their bikes home in the dark. "Okay fellas, let's put your tools away, and then you two need to get going. My guess is your mamm has a meal cookin' for you by now, and you don't want to be late for supper."

Before leaving, Doug and Scott gave their grandpa a hug.

"You two ride your bikes home safely, and danki for your help today. Oh, and don't forget to stop up at the house and let your great-aunt know you're leaving." Eustace peered at Doug and Scott over the top of his glasses.

The boys dashed off to the house, but before they could open the door, Verna stepped out and greeted them on the porch. "You boys be good while I'm away, and always listen to your folks. Hopefully, I'll bring your great-uncle Lester with me on my next visit here." She gave them both hugs.

"Have a nice trip home, Aunt Verna," Doug called as he and his brother mounted their bikes.

"Bye, Aunt Verna." Scott waved at her before the boys peddled down the driveway and onto the road.

Eustace watched his grandsons leave the yard in a matter of seconds. Soon after, Verna popped over to where he and Henry stood, all smiles. "Those are two good boys. I will miss them while I'm away." She sniffed. "Their folks are doing a fine job raising their kinner."

"I can't complain about that. Larry and Arlene have a good group of children, and so do John and Elsie. Except for Joel, my wayward son, I haven't had any problems with my kinner." Eustace glanced down at his worn-out, taped-together boots, before looking back at Verna.

Her eyes filled with tears as she rested her hand on his shoulder. "Keep praying for Joel. Perhaps in time, he will turn his life around."

Eustace could only manage a nod. His throat suddenly felt swollen.

"Well, my friend, shall we call it a day?" Henry stepped up to Eustace and set his hammer on the picnic table.

"Might as well. Let's get the stuff put away." Eustace swatted at a fly buzzing him.

"There's still some coffee left over. Would either of you like a cup?" Verna stood with one hand on her hip.

"No thanks." Eustace shook his head.

"How about you, Henry?" Verna asked.

"Sure, I'll take some to go. Here's my coffee mug." He picked it up from the picnic table and handed it to her.

After Henry helped Eustace put everything away, he grabbed Peaches, carried her over to his tractor, and put the dog inside the pet carrier. When he'd closed it up tight, he checked the bungie straps. "Yep. Everything looks good and secured to travel for my hund. Sure hope she doesn't yelp like a baby all the way home. It can get on a fellow's nerves after a while."

Eustace chuckled. Henry liked to complain about his dog. Truth was, he'd be lost without Peaches.

"Here comes Verna with your coffee." Eustace pointed at his sister.

"Here you go, Henry. I'm not sure when I'll see you again." She handed him the coffee mug.

"Danki. This will be good for the trip home. It's been nice to visit with you, Verna. Eustace, you have a good sister." He took a sip of his coffee.

"I can't complain, Henry. Verna likes to take care of me. No matter how old I get, she still acts like a mother hen whenever she comes around." He chuckled and winked at her. "Guess it's what big sisters do."

She smiled at him.

"Have a safe trip home, Verna. And you'll see me again soon, my friend, Mr. Byler." Henry tugged on Eustace's straw hat. Then he climbed onto his tractor and started it up. Soon, Henry and Peaches were heading down the road toward home.

"I've made turkey sandwiches, and there's some leftover beef vegetable soup I can heat." Verna bumped Eustace's arm with her elbow.

"Sounds tasty. I could handle both of 'em for supper." He stretched and yawned. "What a busy day we've had, jah?"

"It's been busy, all right, but my day isn't over yet. I still need to travel home this evening. I miss Lester and can't wait to see him. Now let's go eat and visit before it's time for me to go." She pushed back a strand of gray hair from her face as they walked together toward the house.

Eustace hated to see his sister go. It would seem lonely without her. But he would do as he'd done since Effie died: keep busy.

Canton, Ohio
When Joel left the jobsite that evening, he pulled out his cell phone to check the time. Eight o'clock. The marriage seminar must be halfway over by now. *I wonder if Kristi's upset with me for not going. She needs to realize my job comes before anything else right now.*

Joel's reasons for not going jabbed his conscience. If he hadn't gotten himself into debt by bidding on the Corvette, he wouldn't be in the position of needing money so badly right now. He'd maxed out his credit cards, too, and didn't dare apply for another one, or he'd really be in over his head.

Joel yawned as he leaned against his truck, watching the sky turn from blue to orange hues. It had been a long day, and the sun was already low in the western sky. He was dog tired, and his body ached from being on his feet all day. His toes cramped inside the confines of his work boots. He couldn't wait to get home to kick them off, take a shower, and relax.

Kristi would have gotten paid yesterday, he thought. *I wonder if she put any money in our bank account. If so, I might be able to take out a bit more.*

Joel admitted he had put himself

at risk taking money from their account the first time. Sooner or later, Kristi was bound to find out what their balance was. Because the statements came to Joel's house didn't mean she wouldn't ask at the bank the next time she made a deposit.

"I'm playing with fire," Joel muttered as he climbed into his truck. "I need a way out, and I need it soon."

Akron

When Kristi got ready to leave the church that evening, she had mixed emotions. While she'd enjoyed the seminar and learned a lot, it wasn't the same without Joel. He needed to hear what the guest speaker said about marriage and the importance of good communication. He'd stressed the need for honesty between a couple and talked about spending quality time together. While Kristi and Joel got together fairly regularly, lately she felt as if his mind was always on other things. The fact that Joel couldn't take a few hours off tonight really bothered her — maybe too much. But couldn't Joel have gone to work earlier this morning so he could attend the seminar?

Kristi was almost to the door when she bumped into her mother. "Oh, sorry. I didn't see you and Dad standing there."

"No harm done." Mom touched Kristi's arm. "Where's Joel? I

thought he was coming with you tonight."

"He was, but he had to work late." Kristi dropped her gaze. She didn't want to let on how disappointed she felt or mention that she thought Joel might have used work as an excuse not to come.

"I'm sorry he couldn't be here," Dad interjected. "He sure missed out on some good stuff."

Kristi held up the packet of information they'd been given, along with the notes she'd taken. "I'll be sharing all the information when I see Joel tomorrow."

"Good to hear." Dad gave Kristi a hug. "If Joel's gonna be my son-in-law someday, then he needs to know how to take care of my daughter."

Avoiding her mother's gaze, Kristi smiled at Dad. "I'm sure he will, Daddy. Joel's a good man."

Chapter 9

Charm

Monday morning, Eustace was up at the crack of dawn. He ate a quick breakfast and got all his outside chores done so he could work on the roof. Several shingles were missing, and with rain in the forecast, he needed to get some patching done or he could be in for a few leaks.

It was a good thing Eustace wasn't afraid of heights, because his two-story house had a steep roof.

He might have asked one of his sons-in-law to help, or even some of the boys, but Eustace enjoyed working and liked to keep busy, so he didn't view it as a chore. He couldn't see asking any of his family for help. They had their own responsibilities to keep up with. This way, he could work at his own pace. Any work he did on this home that he loved so much gave him a sense of satisfaction. At Eustace's age, completing tasks, such as fixing the roof, meant by tonight, every bone in his body would ache. Even so, it was fulfilling to see the results of the work he could still do.

If Effie were here now, she'd be standing beneath my ladder shaking her finger at me and saying I ought to come down and let someone younger take care of this chore, Eustace thought after he'd climbed the ladder and gotten settled on the roof. Of course, Effie had always worried about him, often saying he took too many chances.

Eustace remembered one time he'd made a huge kite, and Effie was sure it would lift him into the air and carry him away. It hadn't, of course, but it probably could have if the wind had been strong enough. *Now, wouldn't that have been something — me sailing through the air like a bird?*

Soon after Eustace became rich, he'd bought a trampoline for his grandchildren to enjoy when they came to visit. Effie was certain it wasn't safe and worried one of the kids might get hurt jumping on it. To put her mind at ease, Eustace had climbed onto the trampoline and jumped as high as he could. When no great tragedy occurred, he even did a few flips. Of course, he'd been a few years younger then. He'd also added a safety net around the perimeter of the trampoline to ensure his grandchildren's protection.

Eustace chuckled as he began patching the roof. As his father used to say, "We only live once, so we may as well have a little fun and take a few chances, or life will become boring."

After he'd worked a while, Eustace began to sweat. *Should have brought some* wasser *up here with me.* He smacked his forehead with the palm of his hand. *Sometimes I can be so forgetful. Guess it comes with age.*

He was about to climb down, when he spotted Elsie's rig coming up the driveway. *Oh, good. I can ask her to get me the water.*

"Hey, Elsie," Eustace called after she'd gotten out of the buggy and secured her horse to the hitching rail. "Would you mind goin' in the house and bringing me a glass of water?"

Elsie looked up, and her mouth opened wide. "What are you doing up there, Dad?"

"Some of the shingles are missing, and I'm replacing them before I end up with a leak in my roof. Since fall is here, we're bound to see more rain."

"John could have replaced shingles for you, Dad. All you needed to do was ask."

"It's okay. I'd rather do it myself. Besides, John's a bricklayer, not a roofer." Eustace chuckled. "That's why so many folks around here call him 'Brick-layer John.' "

"You're not a roofer, either, and you're up so high. What if you fell and no one was here to help?"

Eustace flapped his glove at her. "Stop pestering me. I'm not afraid of heights, and being on the roof is no big deal. I'm perfectly capable of taking care of the job, and I have everything under control. I've done things like this for years. Today is no different."

"But Dad, don't you realize —"

"Are you gonna bring me a glass of wasser or not?"

"Will you come down here to drink it?"

"Why? Are you afraid to climb the *leeder*?"

"No, I am not afraid to climb the ladder." Elsie huffed. "But there's no place to set a glass of water on the roof, now is there?"

"I wasn't gonna set it down. I was planning to drink it."

"Okay," Elsie finally conceded. "I will bring it up the ladder, and then I'll wait there till you drink it."

Smiling, Eustace nodded. "You're

a good daughter. Now hurry inside."

A few minutes later, Elsie returned with a plastic bottle. She made her way up the ladder and handed it to him. "I put water in this bottle instead of a glass. If it gets dropped, it won't break."

Eustace took the bottle, opened the lid, and drank. "Danki. Sure hits the spot." He started to hand it back to her but changed his mind. "Guess I'd better keep the bottle with me in case I get thirsty again."

She remained on the ladder, with lips pursed as she looked up. He figured she was about to plead with him to come down and let John finish the job. So before she could say anything, Eustace spoke. "There's a pile of sullied clothes in my bedroom needing to be washed. Would you mind doing 'em for me?"

Elsie hesitated at first, but finally nodded. "Sure, Dad. I'd be happy to take care of the laundry." She started down the ladder, then suddenly yelled out.

Eustace crawled to the edge of the roof to make sure his daughter was all right. "What happened, Elsie?"

"I missed one of the rungs and almost fell."

"Are you okay?"

"Jah. My legs are kind of wobbly on the ladder right now."

Wiping his brow, Eustace felt relief. Thank goodness she was all right. "I'm holding my end of the ladder till you get down. Now take it slow, one rung at a time." He watched as Elsie went the rest of the way down. What was wrong with him? He should have known better than to ask his daughter to bring him water. Elsie was only forty-two, but it was a risk for anyone climbing a ladder this high. The last thing he wanted was to put any of his loved ones in danger.

Guess I should have been thinking about that the day I asked Elsie to climb the tree and rescue me. But then, Verna went up in the tree house, and so did the boys.

When Elsie's feet touched the ground, she turned and looked up again. "I'll check on you as soon as I get the clothes washed and ready to hang. Please be careful, okay?"

"I'm always prudent."

Elsie shook her finger, reminding him of Effie. "No big words, now, Dad. I want you to take it easy."

Eustace promised. When the screen door shut, he smiled. *Now maybe I can finish my task without interruptions. My daughter means well, but like her mamm, she worries too much. But then, how can I blame Elsie for being concerned? Look what almost happened to her.*

Eustace was nearly finished with his chore when Elsie came out to hang the wet clothes. "How's it going?" she called before heading over to the line.

"Almost done. I'm gonna sit here

a spell and enjoy the sights. You can see forever from up here."

He heard Elsie sigh. Then she headed out to the line and began hanging some towels, as well as his clothes.

Eustace looked out across the pasture, watching his beautiful buggy horse running about in the field. He chuckled as the horse kicked up his heels like a frisky colt and some of the other horses followed, doing the same.

His gaze went to the oil wells, going at a steady speed. *I'm a fortunate man to have all of this.* He drank the last of his water. *Someday, when I'm gone, I hope each of my kinner appreciates what they will eventually receive.*

By the time Eustace climbed down from the roof, Elsie had gone back inside. After putting the ladder and his tools away, he entered the house. When Eustace stepped into the living room, he was surprised to find Elsie going through a stack of mail piled up on an end table near the couch.

"What are you doing?" he inquired.

"I was sorting, to make sure there was no important mail before tossing all the ads and catalogs."

Eustace vigorously shook his head. "No, don't do that! I'm keeping all of those."

She quirked an eyebrow. "Whatever for?"

"I may want to order something.

I've been so busy building the tree house I haven't had time to go through all my catalogs."

Elsie sighed. "Okay, Dad, whatever you want."

Eustace was glad he'd caught her in time. If he'd come in a few minutes later, she may have thrown all the mail in the trash. Then he wouldn't have been able to order anything.

"Say, Dad, it's getting close to noon. Why don't I fix you something to eat?"

"Only if you'll agree to eat with me. It would be nice to have some one-on-one time for a change, and eating by myself is not much fun." Eustace chuckled. "I kinda got used to your aunt's constant chatter."

"Of course I'll stay." Elsie smiled. "What would you like to eat?"

"I'll tell you what. Why don't you make a salad, and I'll grill some steaks? It would be nice to have someone to share the meal with, because I've never gotten used to eating alone."

She gave him a hug. "I understand, which is why I don't understand your insistence on living here by yourself."

"I feel close to your mamm in this home, Elsie. Sometimes, when I look at her rocking chair or some of the clothes she used to wear, I feel like she's still here, watching over me."

"But you know she's in heaven

with God, right? And no matter where you are, whether it's at home or someplace else, she'll always be here."

He nodded as Elsie pointed to her heart. "I look forward to joining her in heaven someday."

Elsie slipped her hand through the crook of Eustace's arm as they walked toward the kitchen. "We don't want it to be anytime soon, which is why you need to be careful."

He patted her hand, thankful for his daughter's love. *Too bad Joel doesn't care much for me. I hope he regrets his actions someday.*

CHAPTER 10

The following morning, after Eustace had enjoyed his first cup of coffee, he opened the back door and stepped onto the porch. The humidity was high, with the smell of rain accompanying a light breeze. Wrinkling his nose, the air actually smelled like earthworms. He glanced at the rocks, where years ago, Effie had meticulously positioned them to border the flowerbed. Her "Suzies" were still in bloom but would soon be dropping their seeds. She always loved those Black-eyed Susans, and now they were Eustace's favorite flower, too. He could see the slimy trails from slugs where they'd crawled across the bordering rocks and into the landscaping. *Guess I better look for something soon to get rid of those slugs before they eat Effie's flowers.*

Eustace leaned forward, holding onto the porch post, and stuck out his hand. For now, only a slight mist fell. He hoped any heavier precipitation would hold off until he got his outside chores done. He also wanted to put finishing touches on his tree house.

Eustace made his way out to the barn to let the horses out to the pasture. As soon as he did, they took off running, kicking, and bucking to the far end of the field. Instead of stopping to graze, they seemed to be a little fidgety as they pranced along the fence row. *Maybe they're feeling their oats, needing to stretch their legs.*

After he made sure the horses' water trough was full, Eustace returned to the barn to clean the stalls. With so much of his time spent building the tree house, he'd neglected some other things.

As Eustace began to muck out the first stall, his thoughts went to Joel. While cleaning had never been Joel's favorite thing to do, he'd always enjoyed spending time with the horses. When Joel turned sixteen, Eustace had given him his first buggy horse. For a year or so afterward, all Joel talked about was Speedy, and how fast he could run. He'd also bragged on his horse, saying the gelding looked finer than any of his friend's buggy horses. Effie used to warn Joel about boasting, and Eustace had as well. But the older their son got, the more he bragged about things. When Joel turned eighteen, he'd bought a car, and everything began to change. He rarely took the horse and buggy out after that, and Speedy didn't seem so special anymore. Joel's convertible became his passion. At first, Eustace figured it was a passing fancy, and when Joel was ready to settle down and join the church, he'd sell the car and that would be the end of it. And it was for a while — until Joel broke poor Anna's heart and took off to seek his fortune in the English world. What a heartbreak it had been for all the family.

By the time Eustace finished cleaning all the stalls, he was sick of reminiscing and more than ready for something to eat. Back in the house, he fixed himself another cup of coffee and set out the cinnamon rolls Doris had brought by last evening on her way home from work. The mere sight and smell of those sweet rolls made his mouth water. He couldn't wait to take his first bite and sip the fresh, hot coffee.

Walnut Creek

As Doris approached the table she would be waiting on, she noticed two little blond-haired girls sitting in high chairs — one on each side of their mother. Dressed alike, and with the same facial features, they were obviously identical twins. The girls looked to be one or two years old, but Doris couldn't be sure. She'd never been good at guessing children's ages.

She was about to ask the young woman if she was ready to order, when one of the little girls started to howl and kick her feet. Patting the child's back, the mother whispered soothing words, but to no avail. The blond-haired cutie continued to cry. Soon, her twin sister followed suit. The poor woman looked fit to be tied. "I'm so sorry," she apologized, looking up at Doris, then quickly glancing around the restaurant. "They're both hungry. We've been out shopping and waited too long to eat."

"Is it all right if I bring them some crackers?" Doris asked. She had done the same thing with fussy children before, and it helped tide them over until their meal was brought out.

The mother smiled. "Oh, would you? If we can get them to stop crying, I can finally order something to eat."

Doris hurried off and returned with several crackers, which she handed to the children's mother.

As soon as the girls were each given one, they stopped fussing and seemed content.

The mother offered Doris a grateful smile. "Thank you. I didn't want them bothering the other patrons."

"You're welcome." As Doris watched the little girls eat, she struggled with feelings of envy. *Why did God bless this woman with two babies when I have none?* She wished she could trade places with the twins' mother. *I need to stop feeling sorry for myself and learn to count my blessings,* she reminded herself. *I have a wonderful husband, five nephews, four nieces, two sisters who are also my best friends, and a father who loves me. There are many people who have no families at all. So with God's help, I will try to remember this and be grateful.*

Smiling, Doris gestured toward the woman's menu. "Are you ready to order now?"

Akron

Kristi scurried about the kitchen, setting the table and stopping to check the crockpot to see if the roast, potatoes, and carrots were done. The aroma coming from the beef caused her stomach to growl. She'd invited Joel to her place for supper this evening and wanted everything to be ready when he got there. She was eager to talk with him about the seminar she'd attended Saturday night.

When Kristi saw Joel on Sunday and gave him a copy of the seminar handouts, along with her notes, he'd promised to look them over once he was settled in for the evening. She was eager to find out what he thought.

Originally, Kristi planned to have Joel over for supper on Monday. But one of the other nurses at the nursing home called in sick, so Kristi worked in her place that evening. It wasn't fun to work two shifts, but others had done it for her when she'd gotten sick, so she felt the least she could do was return the favor. Kristi remembered her grandmother saying that when a person does you a favor, you should pass it on to someone else who has a need.

As she stood there looking at the table, Kristi heard thunder in the distance. "I hope we don't lose electricity." At least the meal she had prepared was already good and hot, so even if the power went out, they'd still be able to eat. "Maybe I better get a few candles out, too. A candlelight dinner might be a nice touch."

Kristi had begun filling the water glasses when the doorbell rang. *Good. Joel's here.* She lit the candles, and after blowing out the match, quickly checked her appearance in the hall mirror and opened the door.

Charm

Eustace had planned to go up in the tree house earlier, but there had been too many interruptions. First, the mail came, followed by paying several bills. Then his friend Henry dropped by and invited him to have lunch at Carpenter's Café, which was upstairs in Keim Lumber. Eustace always enjoyed eating there, so he couldn't say no. Since Henry had driven his tractor over and didn't have Peaches with him, they'd taken Eustace's horse and buggy into town. After their meal, they had stopped by the Shoe and Boot in Charm so Eustace could look for some boots. The ones he'd taped together weren't holding up well, so he figured it was time to get a new pair. By the time they'd come back, Eustace was tired, so as soon as Henry left, he'd laid down on the couch and taken a nap. When he awoke a few minutes ago, he looked out the window, saw the darkening sky, and realized it had started to rain.

He yawned, stretching his arms overhead. "I'm not about to let a little rain keep me from putting a couple of Effie's birdhouses on the railing of my tree house."

Eustace put on his new boots, grabbed his dilapidated straw hat, and headed outside. It was as good a time as any to break in the boots, which right now felt a little stiff. Hopefully, he'd get used to them soon.

The rain came down a bit harder, and clouds blocked out the sun. In the distance he saw a bright flash of lightning and heard the booming clap of thunder, but it was too far away to worry about.

Determined to complete his task, Eustace carried the first birdhouse up the permanently-fixed ladder to the tree house. After nailing it in position on the railing, he stopped and looked toward the west where the storm was slowly approaching. Being up this high, Eustace had a panoramic view, and what he saw made him a little nervous. He noticed a wall of rain like a huge white veil set against the blackened sky, but to him it still looked miles away. Hastily, he went down and got another birdhouse, then came back up. As he anchored the second one in place, the sky opened up in a torrential rain. The wind came in strong and blew Eustace's hat right off his head. Thunder boomed, while a bolt of lightning flashed across the sky.

When Eustace's hair stood straight up, he grabbed his tools. *I'd better get back in the house before lightning comes any closer.* Eustace had heard and read about how when lightning produced electrical charges in the atmosphere before a strike, it could lift a person's hair into the air, providing nature's last warning of a bolt coming out of the blue.

Quickly, he started for the ladder,

but not soon enough. Another jolt of lightning came, this one hitting the tree and engulfing it in the brightest light Eustace had ever seen. Suddenly, it seemed as if everything had slowed down. Then came a sensation of weightlessness, followed by a deafening explosion. His hearing went silent, and as all grew quiet, the last thing Eustace saw was a vision of dear Effie's face.

ABOUT THE AUTHORS

Wanda E. Brunstetter

New York Times bestselling author, Wanda E. Brunstetter is one of the founders of the Amish fiction genre. Wanda's ancestors were part of the Anabaptist faith, and her novels are based on personal research intended to accurately portray the Amish way of life. Her books are well-read and trusted by many Amish, who credit her for giving readers a deeper understanding of the people and their customs. When Wanda visits her Amish friends, she finds herself drawn to their peaceful lifestyle, sincerity, and close family ties. Wanda enjoys photography, ventriloquism, gardening, bird-watching, beachcombing, and spending time with her family. She and her husband, Richard, have been blessed with two grown children, six grandchildren, and two great-grandchildren.

To learn more about Wanda, visit her website at www.wandabrunstetter.com.

Jean Brunstetter

Jean Brunstetter became fascinated with the Amish when she first went to Pennsylvania to visit her father-in-law's family. Since that time, Jean has become friends with several Amish families and enjoys writing about their way of life. She also likes to put some of the simple practices followed by the Amish into her daily routine. Jean lives in Washington State with her husband, Richard Jr. and their three children, but takes every opportunity to visit Amish communities in several states. In addition to writing, Jean enjoys boating, gardening, and spending time on the beach.